BOOK 2 OF THE
MANIFEST DESTINY SERIES

THE NIGHT DOCTOR'S BLADE

JB CAINE AND
BETSEY KULAKOWSKI

BUSY QUILL PRESS

DEDICATION

For Jenny, who braved the rough drafts, cheered for the characters, and reminded us why we write. Thanks for being our partner-in-shenanigans. This one's for you.

CONTENTS

PROLOGUE

IN THE BEGINNING

October, 1942 – Algeciras, Spain

The night air reeked of salt and coal smoke as the last fishing boats drifted back into the harbor. In the hills above the port, the warm yellow glow of oil lamps flickered through shuttered windows of modest homes—quiet, tired places still nursing the wounds of civil war.

Carmen Escaverra wiped the bowls dry and placed them back in the cupboard, then stirred the remaining fish stew so it wouldn't scorch. Satisfied, she began sorting the laundry so that she could soak the blood stains out of her husband's shirt cuffs overnight before washing them in the morning. Her husband Caspar had retired to the parlor to read, exhausted from the daily crises the clinic faced. He'd had to perform an appendectomy today. It hadn't gone as smoothly as it ought to have because supplies were scarce.

The sound of the front door opening and closing made her smile. Her son Esteban came home late again from working the docks. No doubt he was delayed by the foreigners with thick German accents who had taken up in one of the warehouses, always whispering around crates and maps.

"*Hola, mi hijo,*" she called in greeting. A mumbling baritone told her that he'd be intercepted by his father, so she'd have to wait before asking about his day.

The doctor had been watching out the window, waiting for his son to return. This conversation could not wait another day.

"You've been helping the Germans again, haven't you, boy?" An edge of irritation accompanied the question. "I saw you lurking around the warehouses this afternoon."

"And what were you doing by the port this afternoon?" Esteban countered.

"One of the fishermen had a bit of an accident, and don't change the subject."

Esteban sighed, tired of having this same conversation with his father. "The Germans pay good money for a simple task that puts me at no risk. They just want to know which British boats are in the bay and where they are."

"Son, this is not our fight. We have our own problems."

"Exactly. And those problems include not having money or jobs. I don't hear you complaining about the money I bring home when it means an extra pound of beef in our bellies." The young man, not quite 20, set his jaw in defiance and turned back into the hall, headed toward the kitchen where his mother waited with his dinner.

Caspar ran his hand down his face in frustration. The young, they never thought of anything besides the present moment. It was a blessing and a curse at the same time. His thoughts were interrupted by a rumble cutting across the sky. Not thunder, not this time, but the low, rhythmic hum of engines. A British plane, no doubt, flying some mission over Gibraltar. The ground seemed to pause beneath his feet, the very earth holding its breath.

Then the world shattered.

A sound like the sky tearing open cracked above the neighborhood. Blinding, searing light flashed through the window a split second before the shockwave struck. The walls toward the back of the house burst inward. Fire bloomed in the air, and wooden beams split like broken bones. The world moved in slow motion. Screams rent the air over the roar of the blast as half of the house collapsed in a storm of ash and splinters.

Esteban never had time to run.

Across the bay, the British pilot cursed his failing bomber. The Gibraltar cliffs were a shadow in the dark. *Too close!* He had no choice. To avoid crashing into the harbor, he released the payload, sending it to the depths of the sea. He would never know that it struck a quiet coastal neighborhood, not the water.

Caspar only had a heartbeat to throw himself to the ground as the ceiling exploded, glass and timber raining down in a deafening cascade of deadly debris. The air turned to fire and grit. Smoke curled into his lungs. Somewhere nearby, a groan, low and pained, cut through the muffled roar of sound in his damaged ears.

"Esteban!" Caspar coughed, blinking blood and dust from his eyes. Moonlight spilled through the shattered roof, illuminating what remained of the parlor.

His doctor-brain registered the effects of temporary threshold shift, the damage caused to his hearing by the blast. But his father-brain registered another sound. The groan again. Closer now.

The panicked father crawled, pushing aside splintered wood and a broken lamp. In what had been the hallway, he found his son twisted beneath the remains of a support beam. Esteban's face was pale, his lips blue at the corners. Blood soaked through the leg of his trousers, pooling beneath him. The kitchen was gone, and so was Carmen.

"No, no, no ..."

He braced himself and hauled Esteban's limp body through the wreckage, dragging him to the relative shelter of the parlor. He checked for a pulse, for breath. The boy's chest rose and fell, his breathing shallow. Alive, at least for now.

Having been a doctor for 29 years, Caspar had seen the horrors of civil war. He didn't need fancy instruments to know what he faced: internal bleeding, probably a compound fracture, and a wound just above the pelvis that looked like it reached the bone.

He looked around in the destruction, his heart pounding. His medical bag was gone, lost in the rubble. The nearest clinic was miles away, if it even still stood, and the roads would likely be impassible.

Then he saw it: the embroidery frame. His wife's latest work, half finished, lay on the floor, singed but intact. The needle was still threaded with fine cotton floss. *Good enough for sutures.* Crude, but it would hold.

The doctor's gaze flicked up to the mantel above the still-standing fireplace where the shadow box miraculously still hung. Cracked, but not shattered. Inside lay the relic: a narrow-bladed Roman scalpel, its bronze handle fashioned into the shape of a dolphin.

It was a gift from an old colleague in years nearly forgotten, a symbol of a legacy older than borders and bombs.

Now it held Esteban's salvation.

The doctor stood on shaky legs, reached for the box, and smashed the remaining glass with his elbow. He pried the blade from its velvet bed, cradling it with the reverence of a priest holding the sacrament. The blade caught the moonlight—*still sharp.*

He knelt beside his son, whose eyelids fluttered open.

"Papá ..." Esteban whispered, his voice trembling.

"Shh," Caspar soothed. "Stay with me. I need to fix you now."

Esteban's shattered body convulsed with a violent cough, blood spewing from his lips. When he stilled, his breath rattled, wheezy and wet. *Pulmonary hemorrhage.* In a matter of seconds, Esteban might drown in his own blood.

He ripped his son's shirt open and selected an incision point, but a fraction of a second too late. Esteban's frame seized once, then fell silent in death.

No. This cannot be. Driven and unwilling to lose both his wife and his son, Caspar pierced Esteban's skin and muscle deep between two ribs on his left side. Blood seeped from the wound, but the boy's heart had already stopped.

"*Ayúdame,*" Caspar pleaded with the Universe, with God, with whoever in the Cosmos might listen. *Help me.*

And then the impossible happened.

A hum, deep and bone-vibrating, came from the scalpel. A soft golden light bled out from the wound, curling like smoke across Esteban's chest. The air grew heavy ... electric.

He froze, blade in hand. He stared as the blood began to flow *backward*. Veins pulsed and tissue knitted itself back together, leaving only a small cut where the incision had been. The wound in his hip was mending, too, but more slowly.

"Esteban," the father wept.

His son's eyes snapped open—but they were not the same. They were dark mirrors, reflecting a world beyond the living.

"You're alive. You're back. You're safe ..."

But Esteban wasn't listening. His gaze had fixed on the scalpel, humming, pulsing with a heartbeat of its own. He turned to look at the deep cut above his hip, then tilted his head and pressed his fingers inside the wound as far as they would go.

"Esteban, no! You'll get an infection!" It seemed a bizarre warning given the miracle Caspar had just witnessed, but he was still a doctor, after all. He pulled Esteban's fingers out of the gash, not noticing that his son's ring had been lost within.

"You shouldn't have used it," the boy mumbled as the muscles in his face contorted into an empty expression devoid of soul.

They were the last intelligible words he would ever speak.

1

THE TRIAL OF THE WITCH

Present Day – Scottish Highlands

The road to Glen Craeg was little more than a memory etched into the moor, an uneven trail of moss-covered stones swallowed by gorse and peat. The sisters left the car miles behind, trading headlights for torches and the soft crunch of boots against the frostbitten heather.

A low mist clung to the hills, curling around their legs like a living thing. In the distance, the silhouette of the glen yawned wide, cradled by crags like sleeping giants. The ruins of the old witch's croft leaned into the wind near the loch's edge, its crumbling stones slick with time and covered in ivy as thick as secrets.

Somewhere in the distance, a lone curlew cried, long and mournfully, as if echoing a memory. Esme paused, tilting her head.

"You hear that?"

Eliza stilled. It wasn't a bird call. It was a lullaby. Faint. Half-caught in the fog. A tune not sung by any living voice.

Around them, the mist thickened, not with malice but memory. This was sacred ground, where the veil between two worlds thinned. Here, the past wasn't gone. It existed in its many dimensions. The air crackled with old magic that never truly died.

Esme ran her fingers along the edge of the weathered stone wall, etched with ancient runes. Scribbles in some ancient medium—charcoal perhaps—harkened images of dragons and monsters. It told not just of legends, though. It was a sign. A ward. A warning. Or maybe a promise.

Beneath the ruins, the old root cellar waited—a circle of stones sunken into the earth, overgrown and half-buried. A cairn shaped like a sleeping serpent, marked the entrance. The home of Morag, the Widow of the Glen.

The missing artifact, the *Last Dragon's Egg*, might be kept here, if anywhere still held its warmth. But they'd need to earn the old widow's trust. Glen Craeg did not give up its ghosts, or its dragons, easily.

The sisters stood before the serpent cairn, their torches scanning the moss-slick stones for signs of a hidden door or secret niche. Esme crouched beside a tuft of something growing in the dark recesses of the root cellar. Beneath it, carved into the foundation, a mosaic of obsidian scales twisted in a spiral pattern. Some were missing, others dulled with age. At its center, a shallow bowl etched with ancient runes and a glowing symbol that resembled a dragon's eye.

Eliza knelt beside it, wincing as pain tugged the muscles in her neck. Her injured throat would not allow her to speak, not properly, not since Maelis's blade had silenced her. *Had it been a year?* Instead, she traced the edge of the bowl with two fingers, brows furrowed. Her breath steamed in the morning air, but her focus remained unshaken.

Esme watched her. "It's a song puzzle," she murmured. "A lullaby ... Morag's lullaby." Eliza glanced up, nodding, a smile brightening her typically stoic face. "Maybe the only way to awaken the widow is to sing her song?"

Eliza nodded. She pointed to Esme, then to the bowl. *You have to sing.* Eliza's eyes spoke the words she could not.

Esme swallowed hard. "Me? I don't know the song."

Eliza tapped her temple, then placed her hand on Esme's chest. She closed her eyes and drew in a breath. *You do. It flows through you.* Forcing it, Eliza managed a faint hum in a tune Esme almost remembered, like a ghost from their childhood. Then it came to her, the crackling voice of their Scottish grandmother.

The tune was one not just every Scot knew, but one almost everyone on the planet recognized. It was a song that united nations and spoke of happier times—a song sung every year, like clockwork, to harken in the new year. But Esme remembered the version their grandmother sang.

She paused to clear her throat, aware of what Eliza's must feel like as nerves gripped her like a hand tightening around her neck. She took a deep breath and let her voice be guided by her memories of her maternal grandmother, a Lady of the Armstrong clan.

Hush now, my wee one, close yer eyes.
The stars are climbin' high.
The heather dreams beneath the moon,
And so, my love, shall I.

The tentative timbre of her song faded, as the beauty of her voice reverberated off the stones. The acoustics of the chamber put the Aldwych Theatre to shame. It gave Esme courage to continue.

Lie still, my flame, the night is kind,
The mist guards every glen,
And should ye wake, I'll sing again,
'Til day returns, amen.
No hunter's horn shall stir ye sleep,
No storm nor shadows grim,

For while I breathe, ye're safe wi' me,

In earth, in sky, and hymn.

The glow of the dragon eye in the stone strengthened, throbbing with a heartbeat that matched the tempo. Eliza encouraged Esme to continue, as if a conductor's baton guided her hand. Eliza tried to sing along, but her voice wouldn't cooperate, and it sounded more like a croaking toad than a song. It didn't stop her from trying, if only in whispers.

So dreams of flight 'bove loch and brae,

O' winds that rise and turn,

And shall I keep yer ember bright,

'Til fire and soul return.

Those were the words Esme intended to sing, but those were not the words that came from her mouth. Instead, the words slurred into something more, *dragon-like.*

Zar drāvak ir'syl thurin'kaar,

Vel'kyn drōmah zhelen,

Aruv zharneth kal-drien far,

Tal shur vakaar en'en.

The runes carved into the walls, even those worn by time, flickered to life, casting a puce glow in the dark cellar. The mosaic began to turn, clicking as the pieces shifted into different places. A low rumble echoed beneath their feet.

Suddenly, the mist above the cairn coalesced, gathering and twisting until it formed the ghostly image of a woman. Majestic. Ancient.

Eliza looked up, her breath catching. The vision of Morag gained her physical form. She was slight, but sound, her eyes bright but cautious. Her long white locks were knotted and twisted into braids and cords, charms tied into the tresses. She wore a dark gown from a long forgotten time with a swatch of plaid pinned over her shoulder. The Widow inspected the girls, then bowed not to Esme, but to Eliza.

Behind the witch, where the dim light only caught her silhouette, stretched the impossible shadow of something else entirely. A great serpent, crowned and coiling, its massive body breaching the shimmering light like the Monster, broke the surface of the nearby loch. It was not a shadow, nor a trick of the mist. It was truth made visible.

The witch's voice echoed across the glen, not with sound, but with memory. A single word settled into their minds:

"Prove."

Then the cairn slid open with a hiss of displaced air, revealing a chamber lit with bioluminescent moss which grew on the walls, and up a single pedestal. Upon it rested an egg as large as a pumpkin, shimmering with iridescent scales, and pulsing with life.

Before they could take it, Morag stepped into their path, her voice deeper now.

"Only one may carry it. The one who remembers fire."

Eliza closed her eyes. She felt the burn of the Covenant's ritual, the sear of the blade, and the moment death kissed her and left her changed.

Esme reached for the egg, then paused. "It's you, isn't it?" she whispered. "She means *you*."

Eliza nodded, trembling. Her fingers hovered just above the shell, warmth radiating from within. She remembered fire. And so did the egg.

Dragons? Why dragons? When their instructors told them there would be a test before they graduated from the Academy, she hadn't expected a live-action simulation. Once she understood the intent, she expected a *real-world* scenario. She expected to make decisions and take actions based on their weapons training, logistics, spy-craft and the science of human behavior, all topics that had been covered in great detail over the past year.

This was too surreal, like a storybook brought to life. It felt more like a simulation in a holodeck, or the *Kobayashi Maru* from Star Trek. Would this be a *no-win* situation?

She had a flash of memory, watching the show with Elias when they were children. It was their favorite. The thought of her brother, however, came and went like the tide. Her mind went back to the *Kobayashi Maru* she was certain she now faced.

The weight of it burned in her chest. Eliza's throat grew tighter with every breath. Still, she had no choice. She had to proceed with the *mission* to its inevitable end.

Her hand contacted the shell, but rather than burn, it warmed her to the core, the chill of an October night forgotten. It hummed, and Eliza became aware of the pulsing heartbeat within.

A deep, seismic thrum echoed through the chamber. The ground heaved beneath them. Rocks tumbled from the reinforced walls. Eliza caught the egg as the pedestal beneath it folded open like a blooming flower. She held it like a mother with a newborn as the chamber shifted. Stone ground against stone. The runes flickered on the walls, racing, not in warning, but in judgement.

Esme stumbled back as the mist coalesced again, this time forming a draconic figure, spectral and ancient. It was not hostile, but it was watching. This echo of a dragon appeared nothing like the CGI-generated *Smaug* portrayed in *The Hobbit*. This dragon was more delicate, more Celtic. He loomed above them as the ceiling of the chamber seemed to rise, or perhaps the floor lowered. His eyes were soft, filled with recognition.

Eliza clutched the egg to her chest just as the floor fell out from beneath them. A hidden pit yawned wide. But instead of plummeting, they were caught midair, by a column of golden swirling light.

The runes spiraled around Eliza like living ink, crawling across her skin. The egg pulsed against her heart. The wound inside her throat began to burn. Not with pain, but with heat, as though the fire of the dragon poured into her.

The voices of the spectral witch and dragons spoke as one:

"This is your trial. Your test. One must be forged anew to carry fire. Flesh must remember death. But the soul must choose to live."

Flames erupted around the edge of the pit. It burned, but Eliza was not consumed. The flames moved to form a circle. Esme rushed forward, but the flames pushed her back. She wanted to aid her sister, still fragile from her recent death and resurrection. She wanted to bear the burden of carrying the egg. Eliza had been through enough already.

Like Frodo bearing the ring to Mordor, Eliza hadn't been the same since leaving the Nest last November. Like Samwise, Esme would have borne each of her sister's struggles, if only for a little while.

Esme felt a tremor as her gift awakened. The shadow of the vision world into which she often crossed came over her, and she watched the Widow of the Glen place the egg deep into the earth, away from the eyes of men who lusted for the power it might offer. She saw the memory of the young dragon as he nuzzled Esme's cheek with his horn, distraught that its clutch-mate had not hatched. Then she saw the moment of her sister's death, crimson against the glint of Maelis's blade. Clarity came when she focused on the blade and recognized the shape as the dragon's horn. She saw the haze of blood. Gushing. Spurting. Spraying.

Then there was something else. There was a burst of light, and a heartbeat not her own. The chamber rumbled again, and the egg cracked, ever so slightly. The hairline fracture allowed the light within to illuminate the darkness.

A piercing screech like a newborn baby's cry echoed around them, and Esme came out of the world of shadows to see her sister cradling the new life in her arms. The dragonling gazed into Eliza's eye with a look of wonder, its first moments in the world as traumatic as Eliza's last.

Esme took a tentative step toward the creature that looked so sweet and innocent. It hiccupped. A puff of smoke billowed from its nostrils. Esme stepped back, matching gazes with Eliza.

"How come *you* get to be the Mother of Dragons?" A hint of envy painted Esme's tone.

"That is because it is her test alone, Esme." A familiar male voice came from behind them. Eliza gazed up and saw Solan Virell, the Grand Aegis of the Order, squatting down over the collapsed cairn. "Well done. Normally, we would begin Esme's trial right away, but we don't have the luxury."

"Wait." Esme moved closer to her sister, but the dragon nipped at her, and she recoiled, hopping away from danger. "I thought this was *our* trial."

"Each acolyte must face their own test, Esme," he said, coming down the steps that neither of the girls had noticed. "Eliza is a woman of science. Her test required her to step outside of the world she knows. To have faith in science but believe in the unbelievable. It also shows her trust in others, particularly in you, Esme. As her field partner, and younger sister, she needs to allow you to lead when she cannot."

Eliza had to allow that his logic was sound. In the past, she'd have told her sister what to do, but her current limitations prevented it.

"But your test will have to wait, Esme. We just received word that one of our Agents has found something significant in Romania. We need to provide support, and the High Council agrees you are the right ones for the job. Randall said he'd be happy to watch Faraday while you're away."

Solan paused, turning to the Widow who stood with an expression that suggested she was put off by his sudden arrival. "Sorry to cut the show short, love." He addressed her with a familiarity of old friends. "The girls are needed elsewhere. Are you satisfied?"

"*Auch aye*," the woman said, picking up the broken egg, closing it. The dragon in Eliza's arms disappeared, startling her.

"Wait. What?" Esme gasped. Eliza didn't look any less confused.

Morag moved closer to Solan, running her hand along his cheek. "Dinnae ferget tae bring the haggis fer Burn's Night. Will I see ye then?"

"Yes, of course," Solan leaned in and kissed her cheek.

"Thank you for your help, again," he said, turning back to the girls. "As I was saying ..."

The vision of the hidden cairn faded into nothingness, and with it, the Widow of the Glen and her egg were gone.

Eliza put a hand in the middle of Solan's chest, lifting her hand into an arc, questions filling her eyes.

"Oh, well," he said, "we have a formal alliance with certain individuals to aid in testing our new acolytes. Morag, well, she's a fine auld girl." His Scottish accent wasn't all that convincing. "There are those with true magic, and we're lucky she works for us."

Eliza shook her head and turned away, done with the whole affair.

"When do we leave?" Esme asked.

"Charmaine is making arrangements for a flight this evening," he said. "You have a few hours to get something to eat, sleep, shower, whatever you need. There'll be a full briefing before you go."

Eliza tapped her wrist as if she wore a watch, then lifted her hands in question.

"I know it's not much time," Solan said, "but if the *Healer's Shard of Arkanos* falls into the hands of the Covenant it won't be good. Any relic that ancient likely has tremendous power. We suspect it was in the Manifest, based on some of Christopher Wren's notes. While we don't know what it does, it might unleash a plague on mankind. It could mean the slaughter of millions. By the time anyone sees what is happening, the rot will have set in, and no doctor in the world can cut it out."

2

ECHOES OF SILENCE

"Eliza." Solan stood in the doorway of his office, motioning for her to follow. Eliza glanced back at her half-eaten food and decided she wasn't hungry after all. Esme had eaten and sacked out on a sofa by the fireplace. It took Eliza longer to eat these days. She had to take small bites, chew carefully, then hope to swallow with the ever-present lump in her throat.

"What is it?" she said, forcing the words.

"Standard practice," he answered. "I'm sure you understand. You'll need a physical before we send you into the field."

"Seems like ... an after ... thought, sir."

"Perhaps," he said. "But Dr. Yang has some concerns. For your safety."

Eliza had met Dr. Ling Mai Yang at one of her parents' dinner parties, and any protests were lost. She liked the woman who wasn't more than 10 years her senior. She nodded to Solan, who led her to the lift and down to a floor she'd never visited.

The walls were a relaxing pale blue, the tile floors white with flecks of mica that glinted gold in the harsh lighting. The hallway wasn't unlike the hall to her lab, but this felt more ... sterile.

Halfway down the corridor, he stopped and opened the door, holding it for her, allowing Eliza to pass. Dr. Yang sat at a desk with a laptop computer and a medical file. She glanced up when they entered, and her stern expression softened into a genuine smile.

"Dr. Wren," she beamed, standing, offering a hand. "It's good to see you."

"Likewise," Eliza replied, taking the seat the physician motioned to.

"Mission briefing at 4:00," Solan said. "See you then." She glanced over her shoulder as Solan stepped out, leaving them in respect of Eliza's privacy.

"It's been a few years," she said. "How are your parents?"

"Well," she croaked, swallowing hard. A sense of dread washed over her, the fear of a protracted conversation made her uncomfortable. She didn't have the energy to squander on chit-chat.

Dr. Yang seemed to sense the issue. "So, I've been looking over your chart. You had quite a scare." Eliza nodded. "How are you doing these days? Still some issues with your voice?"

"Yes," Eliza said. She wanted to say so much more, but it was too much work.

Dr. Yang studied her. "Any issues swallowing? Eating?"

Eliza nodded.

"Sleeping okay?"

Eliza lifted a shoulder non-committally. "Didn't sleep well ... before."

"Nightmares? Flashbacks?"

Eliza paused, debating how much to tell her. She shook her head no. She wasn't ready to talk about the nightmares. "Not really."

Dr. Yang made notes. "Well, since I know you're on a tight schedule, I've called in the team to run you through all the usual tests. So, a lot is going to happen in the next few hours. We'll draw blood, run some scans, and conduct an examination by laryngoscopy. I have a trauma-informed therapist on staff that I'd like you to talk to about your mental health, because we want all our Agents to be of sound mind. She'll be available to you as one of your employee benefits, so if I may recommend, build a firm foundation of trust. I think you'll find her to be a trusted confidante."

Eliza swallowed hard but nodded. She'd stopped listening after the word laryngoscopy. She'd endured one while still in hospital, and it'd been dreadful. She'd rather have her teeth yanked without anesthetic than go through that again.

"Let's get started."

True to her word, Dr. Yang ran her through the full gamut of tests, including a CT scan of her brain, an electroencephalogram, spirometry, and the dreaded scope through her nose, which wasn't as bad as it had been at the hospital in London.

She talked to the counselor and a speech-language pathologist who conducted a swallow test. He evaluated her for an electrolarynx or resonance device, but decided it might be premature since she was still able to produce sound.

The clock read 3:27 when she returned to Dr. Yang's office, feeling as if she'd been through the wringer, leaving her out of sorts and exhausted. She hadn't finished her breakfast, and she was hungry.

She had to wait while Dr. Yang studied the test results that had been processed with an efficiency that public medicine couldn't reproduce.

When she finally turned from the computer, the doctor's expression was as blank as the wall behind her. Panic rose in her chest. A look of disappointment might have been more comforting than the placid emptiness in Dr. Yang's dark eyes.

"That bad?" she managed.

"Not as bad as I expected," Ling Mai said. "The scar tissue is clean. No adhesions, no granulomas. Structurally, your vocal cords are ... remarkably intact."

Eliza arched her brow. Her throat constricted out of reflex.

"I know what you're thinking," Dr. Yang said. "You should be able to speak. Physically, everything is in place. But it would seem the nerves aren't firing as they should. It's like someone rewired the circuit board, but the power source isn't properly connected." It made more sense when the doctor put it in engineering terms.

The words were there. She could speak them, but she couldn't muster the force needed to expel them. *Worst case of laryngitis ever.*

"There's something else," Ling Mai said. "Your electroencephalogram showed something ... *unusual.* There's a mild interference in your brain waves I've never seen before."

"Am I ... am I going ... crazy?" Eliza asked. After *the incident,* she'd considered the fact that hearing voices whispering as she was falling asleep might be a problem, but now the whispers were so frequent they'd become a constant companion.

"Your psychological profile is strong, considering what you endured," the doctor said. "But I'd be lying if I said your brain scans weren't strange. Whatever they did in that ritual, whether it was the Veil or the fact that you technically died, it changed you."

Eliza's eyes closed. *Who wouldn't be changed by death?*

Now and then, the words of the ritual rose again, half in Latin, half in something older. *Umbrae vocem audite ... anima fracta, redi ad nos...Umbrae vocem audite ... Mortui te exspectant.*

"Psychologically, you're high-functioning. You're coping, but there are markers. It's evident in the sleep disturbances, elevated cortisol, and isolated neural spikes in your temporal lobe." She reached a hand across the desk to Eliza, who fought the urge to pull away. "Eliza, I know this is hard. You're not going *crazy*. You're not *broken*. But you are ... *changed*. That's harder, but it's survivable."

Their eyes met, and Eliza felt something akin to relief. She wasn't *crazy*. She was *changed*. There was a difference.

"We'll continue to monitor," she said. "When you get back from your trip, Dr. Davenport will begin speech therapy and rehabilitation with you. It may take time, but with treatment, there is hope for your voice to return. We'll address the sleep and mental strain issues, too. For now, avoid straining your voice as much as possible. I would advise a few additional items for your field kit."

"Like what?" Eliza croaked.

"Little things. A whistle, so you can alert others to danger without shouting, lozenges to soothe your throat, and a resonance mic for any radio systems you may be assigned to use. I'd prescribe some mild sleeping pills, but I suspect you won't take them."

Eliza shook her head no. The doctor shrugged and sat back in her chair.

"I'll include the equipment suggestions in the report for Solan. Which, by the way, will not include any medical information other than a go/no-go status, along with recommendations for accommodations and equipment. Your medical information is confidential and will remain as such."

"Go ... or no-go?" Eliza asked, still not sure of the verdict.

"Go," Dr. Yang said, then stood. "And you have a meeting to get to."

"Thank you." Eliza stood, gave her a nod, and made a hasty retreat.

The table was circular, deliberately so. No one sat at the head. A wall of antique maps had been overlaid on a clear plexiglass screen with digital grids. Illuminated markings glowed around its edge, casting a pale blue glow across the faces around the table. Solan Virell stood with his hands behind his back, posture rigid but voice calm. He cut an imposing figure with kind features but stern mannerisms. His suit was impeccably tailored, his beard neatly trimmed.

Eliza sat with her arms crossed, and the neck of her sweater hid the scar that bisected her throat. Her stomach growled, and her eyelids were heavy for want of sleep. Beside her, Esme was alert, silent, hanging on every word. She seemed excited to finally have a mission to participate in. They'd been training for this day for eleven months, but to Eliza it seemed rushed. Premature.

Why us? The words kept running through her mind. *Why now?*

Solan tapped the clicker in his hand with his thumb as Charmaine entered the room and set a cup of fancy craft-brew coffee in front of him before taking her seat. Her lips tightened to a thin line as she settled into her chair at Solan's left and gazed up at the screen.

A grainy satellite image of the Carpathian Mountains flickered into view, then zoomed in on a small town in the eastern central region of Romania. "This is the Zlatna Central Recovery Hospital," he said. "Abandoned since 1982. Officially, it served as a wartime hospital and long-term psychiatric facility for Romanian soldiers. Unofficially ..."

The silence hung heavy in the room until Esme leaned toward Charmaine and touched the pendant hanging around her neck. "Oh, how lovely! Is that a ruby nautilus? It's so unusual to see red used for sea-related jewelry. You'd usually see something in hues of blue or green, and—"

"Thank you," Charmaine interrupted quickly, noting Solan's disapproving eye. "It was a gift from my grandmother. Please continue, sir."

Solan cleared his throat in annoyance as Esme, thus chastised, sat back in her chair. "... it was a black op site. Used by the Covenant under the protection of Nazi SS researchers. Possibly even under the direct influence of the Ahnenerbe."

Someone at the table muttered a curse.

"What's the Ahnenerbe?" Esme asked innocently.

"A pseudoscientific organization founded by the Schutzstaffel in Nazi Germany in 1935," Charmaine explained. "Established by Heinrich Himmler himself." As Solan's administrative assistant, she'd immersed herself in research for the briefing. She always seemed to know at least as much as her boss did.

"Oh," Esme seemed to sink into her chair.

Solan continued. "Aegis Field Agent Dr. Phillip Thorpe has been working in the region for several years, assigned to work with archeology teams while monitoring the area for signs of Covenant activity. The team discovered an abandoned tunnel beneath the hospital, partially collapsed in one area, then bricked shut. After excavating it ..." he seemed to hesitate, which snapped Eliza out of her misery.

Who held a meeting without offering refreshments? She cast an envious eye at Solan's coffee. She'd kill for a cuppa and a scone.

"We recovered a black military service tag," Solan tapped his controller again, and the map faded, replaced by the image of a black metal circle stamped with lettering. Numbers curved along the bottom edge, but the lettering was unmistakable.

"Wren?" Esme gasped, and Eliza sucked in a breath.

The temperature in the room seemed to drop and a chill washed through Eliza. The voices in her head silenced, which added to her sense of dread.

Eliza's finger pointed back to herself, then to Esme.

"Yes." Solan seemed to sense her question without her having to ask it. "Corporal Alban Wren served as a medic, but also an Agent of Aegis during World War II. He was a part of a top-secret operation called *Operation: Grimwell*. He monitored Covenant activity in Hungary. Several months into the operation, his unit was attacked. Whether it was Nazi, Turkish, Russian, or Covenant Forces, we can't be certain. The British Army listed missing in action in 1944, a year and one day later, his status changed to *presumed killed in action*."

"How are we related to him?" Esme asked.

"He's your father's great-uncle," Solan said.

"Father never mentioned him," Esme said. "Not that I recall."

"I'm surprised you've never heard his name. He was an exceptional Agent, and while the Covenant didn't work directly with the SS that we know of, they monitored their activities, as did Aegis. Several of their weapon technologies were *intercepted*, shall we say?"

"What?" Eliza asked.

"Examples? I'll tell you, but this is confidential information that does not leave this room."

The girls nodded.

"Hitler had plans to bomb New York," he said. "We know that from the work of Agents like young Corporal Wren. They infiltrated the Nazis and collected reconnaissance. Hitler obsessed with taking out lower Manhattan and building a long-range bomber capable of delivering a payload and returning to the European mainland. The *Amerikabomber* was one of the many initiatives of the *Reichsluftfahrtministerium*, or the Ministry of Aviation, if your German is lacking."

He must have seen Eliza's engineering-mind at work. "Yes, that is a round trip distance of 11,600 kilometers and the Nazis didn't have aircraft capable of delivering a payload that far."

"What kind of payload would that take?" Esme wondered aloud.

Eliza reached for the pen in front of her and did some complex calculations quickly.

4.5 to 5 tonnes. She circled the answer.

"At one point, the Portuguese Prime Minister allowed naval ships to refuel at the islands, so the Germans decided that would be an ideal launching point for the *Amerikabomber*."

"But it never happened."

"Yes, due in part to work done by Aegis agents like Corporal Wren."

"So, what is ... *Operation: Grimwell*," Eliza asked.

Solan glanced away for a moment. "During the second World War, there was an *incident*." He swallowed hard. "The RAF sent a squadron of bombers over Germany to identify a factory used to manufacture an alleged weapon called *Die Glocke*, or *Wunderwaffe*. If the *Amerikabomber* was infeasible, then the *Wunderwaffe* might be equal to the task. The Third Reich intended to end the war and dominate the world. The rumors spread Hitler wanted to test it on London first."

Eliza's brow lifted and Esme gasped.

"*Operation: Grimwell* meant to put a stop to that plan. Unfortunately, the planes took heavy flack as they made their escape from Germany. One veered off course over Spain and accidentally dropped its last remaining bomb on Algecira. Many died. The RAF sent aid, including Alban Wren. Alban was our man on the inside. While he was there, the Order asked him to look for an item we had tracked from Sir Christopher Wren's notes. We suspected the item—*The Artifact of Arkanos*—was in the region based on a sales slip from an antiquities dealer."

"Is there any chance he might be alive? After all these years?" Esme asked, her brow furrowed with concern, but her eyes alight with hope.

Solan considered her question for a moment. Eliza thought he seemed hesitant to answer. "That would be ... *unlikely*, given the number of years that have passed," he finally said.

Lifting his hand before any other questions could be fired at him, he continued. "I understand what this suggests, but I caution everyone. This is not a recovery mission. We are not pursuing legends or ghosts. This is fact-finding only."

Esme looked at her sister, questioning gazes passing between them.

Solan met Eliza's gaze when she turned back to face him. "We've arranged for you to meet with Dr. Thorpe. He specializes in historical forensics and artifact-related anomalies. He'll provide local context and help guide this investigation."

He paused, seeming to choose his words with great care.

"What we find may challenge what we understand about *Grimwell* and the Covenant's role in the war, if I'm being honest." Eliza believed him, but suspected he held something back. "But we do not go in assuming the worst. Or the ... impossible."

He looked directly at Esme this time.

"You're to document everything. No assumptions. No engagement unless authorized. We owe Corporal Wren the respect of truth and closure for your family as to his fate."

"Are we ... expecting ... *resistance*?" Eliza's voice caught in the question.

Solan considered her for a moment. "No," he said. "I haven't heard anything from Dr. Thorpe to suggest that. The region is ... *untidy*. We don't know if there are still Covenant operatives and possible artifacts hidden in old buildings and abandoned mine shafts. Without the Manifest, it's hard to know what we might find, but the region is rife with legend. Old ghosts. Ancient secrets."

Another beat passed.

"Gear up," Solan finally said to Esme and Eliza. "You don't have much time until your flight. Charmaine will help you build your field kits before you go."

Will there at least be snacks on the plane? Eliza wanted to ask, but said nothing.

Eliza knew about field kits. Some of the equipment Agents carried in the field were her inventions. She didn't know what kind of equipment she and Esme might need, for an operation of this type. If they were just collecting data, she might need nothing more than a notepad and a pen. She already had those.

Charmaine led them to another room where a duffle bag had been prepared for each of them. All agents carried some of the same basic items, but there were options laid out for them based on personal preferences.

"I'll need your cell phones, please," Charmaine addressed them with an air of formality. "You'll be issued new phones, but your personal devices cannot be allowed to go with you."

"What if mother and father need to reach us?" Esme said, reaching into her pocket for her phone.

"Your parents know you're being deployed, and that you will be *absum* for at least a week, possibly longer."

"Faraday?" Eliza choked on the word. She always worried about her cat.

"He's staying with Randall, remember?" Esme said, nudging her.

Eliza was too tired to function. "Will Randall pick him up?"

"It's already been taken care of. Don't worry about your cat. I think Faraday and Tiberius will get along famously," Charmaine beamed.

Eliza nodded begrudgingly, wishing the cat could go with them, but she acknowledged that would not be practical.

Charmaine smiled, her eyes atwinkle. "Now, let's talk about travel plans."

3

THE SANATORIUM'S SECRETS

Tall pines swayed like mourners in the moonlight as Dr. Phillip Thorpe picked his way down the overgrown trail, a canvas satchel slung over his shoulder and a flashlight gripped in his hand. The dig site lay quiet. The graduate students, who were also Aegis trainees, and local laborers lay fast asleep in their tents, exhausted from a week of excavation.

But Thorpe couldn't sleep. Not after what they'd found. He knew he should wait for the Order Agents to arrive, but the infernal *wondering* burned in his brain. Why had the box of personal trinkets been in the half-buried tunnel? How were these items, or the people who owned them, connected to the *Spitalul de Recuperare Zlatna*, the ironically-named Zlatna Central Recovery Hospital? And how did the identification tags of a British soldier and member of the Aegis Order who disappeared 80 years ago end up in Romania?

He paused at the edge of a clearing, just outside the perimeter of what had once been the grounds of the sanatorium that, according to locals, had a less-than-sterling reputation for "treating" patients with a variety of mental illnesses. The long-abandoned building loomed in the woods like a rotting memory. Its walls were cracked and vine-choked, and many sections had collapsed decades ago.

Still, the structure refused to die, much like the rumors that surrounded it. Rumors of voices in empty corridors, of doors that opened and closed on their own, of phantom lights in the vacant windows. And older still, rumors of soldiers brought here at the end of the war who were never seen again.

Thorpe's breath fogged as he summoned his courage and made his way across the weedy lawn. The door hung at an awkward angle, evidence that local kids had come here on a dare, or to engage in shenanigans their parents wouldn't appreciate. He made a mental note to keep an eye out for any such wayward teenagers, or even vagrants who might be squatting here.

The autumn chill descended as he stepped inside. His flashlight beam flicked across shattered windows, iron railings, and stained concrete. Somewhere beneath this structure, the tunnel ran. And within that tunnel, or perhaps within the decaying building itself, lay clues to solving a decades-old mystery for which an Order Agent likely gave his life.

He reached a breach in the stone floor where a section had caved in, a result of an earthquake in the region during the 90s after the place had been deserted. A rope ladder had been tied to one of the staircase railings, indicating that someone had ventured into the fissure to investigate. He tugged on the rope and found it solid, despite being exposed to the elements for a number of years.

"I must be out of my fool mind," he muttered to himself as he picked his way down, his boots crunching on loose stone.

At the bottom, he moved forward, panning his light over what appeared to be a sub-basement used for maintenance offices and storage in years past. He followed the concrete hallway, noting a variety of graffiti of all the standard types, left by tourists and local looky-loos.

Andrei a fost aici și a supraviețuit! Andrei was here and survived!

Mortul te așteaptă. The dead are waiting for you.

Suntem toți greșiți aici. We're all wrong here.

Just the kinds of messages one might expect to find in an abandoned asylum full of ghost stories. After years of working with the Order, he'd seen his share of hauntings, and he had to concede the fact that this place had an unsettling vibe, even for a building riddled with residual haunts—spectral images that played over and over like a phantasmagoric highlight reel of tragedy.

He cursed his impulsivity for coming alone and not alerting anyone about his plans. No wonder he had the reputation of being a bit of a reckless cowboy. He was incredibly good at his triptych of a job as a linguist, a scholar, and a field agent, though, so his handlers were willing to accept a little foolhardiness and write it off to bravery.

He knew better, though. It was curiosity, simple as that.

His flashlight illuminated a T-intersection, and after a moment's deliberation, he turned toward the direction of the dig site, hoping to find the other end of the mysterious tunnel. The darkness here was complete, any ambient light from the moon extinguished this deep into the bowels of the basement.

His years in jungles and subterranean ruins earned him an excellent internal compass, and when he came to a service passage, he knew he'd found what he sought. The walls were slick with condensation, and his superior sense of smell alerted him to the scent of mildew. It took him a moment of rooting around in his pack, but his fingers eventually brushed against the rough texture of the construction-grade respirator mask. He snapped off the light for a moment as he secured the protective gear over his nose and mouth.

The inky blackness enveloped him, and Phillip used the opportunity to listen to the sounds of the sanatorium. But there weren't any. None of the *drip drip drip* he expected. No scurrying of creatures or fluttering of bats, despite the sickly sweet scent of guano lingering in the air. The silence was oppressive.

And then he heard it.

A faint and irregular drag, like boot heels scraping across stone with uneven steps.

He froze.

Then another sound, coiled through the darkness like smoke: a raspy whisper like a shallow sigh.

He fumbled to turn the light back on, its beam flickering as though resisting any disturbance to the perfect dark. But in its reluctant beam, he caught a glimpse of something in a doorway ahead of him to his right.

A figure.

Pale and grey, wearing a tattered tee shirt that might once have been white and dingy khaki pants with large exterior pockets. At first, Phillip thought he'd found a squatter, but as the figure raised its milky eyes into the full glow of the beam, the archaeologist thought he was in a Boris Karloff movie. The man was impossibly gaunt, his skin taut and pulled back away from his mouth and eyes.

A mummy!

But it wasn't a mummy, because it was moving. Its jaw creaked open, emitting a sound that Dr. Thorpe could best equate to shuffling old parchments, age-worn and dusty. He should be panicking, running, but his body wouldn't move, the way one can't run away in a nightmare.

He hadn't been prepared for how fast the *thing* moved.

The flashlight clattered to the ground and rolled across the hallway, creating a dim light as the Agent and the creature struggled. For being little more than a corpse, it was strong, but not superhumanly so, and Phillip's years of aikido training gave him grappling skills for which he was infinitely grateful in this moment.

He stepped back and raised his arms, slipping out of the monster's hold. When it lunged at him again, Phillip swooped his right leg behind his attacker's and executed a spinning *irimi nage* throw in an attempt to bring his opponent to the ground.

It didn't lose balance, though.

Instead, it slipped up behind him and punched him in the kidney with its bony fist. Pain shot through Phillip's back. He grunted, his knee buckling just enough to give the *thing* an advantage.

An advantage it took.

It kicked the back of Phillip's knee, sending him to the ground, then pounced on him like a lion on its prey. They pitched and rolled, fighting for purchase and leverage over each other.

Phillip's practices with Sensei Arakawa came back to him.

Flow with your opponent.

No punching, no kicking. Just break the bones and go home.

He scrabbled around and got the creature in a shoulder lock, hoping to take a moment to catch his breath while his enemy was pinned. But with a loud *pop*, it dislocated its own shoulder to break his hold.

The *thing* got to its feet, its right arm hanging limp at its side, attached only by grey skin and sinew. It prepared to charge again.

"What are you?" Phillip yelled as he ripped off the N-95 mask that had slid over to his cheek. The sound of his voice caused the *creature* to hesitate for just a moment. Phillip took advantage, leaping forward and closing the distance between them. He drove his fingertips into the tender skin just below the ribs.

To Phillip's horror, the desiccated flesh tore, and he found himself wrist-deep in the *thing's* abdomen.

It seemed to register no sensation of pain, and instead clamped its left hand around Phillip's throat. It began to squeeze.

As he began to pull his hand out of the *thing's* abdomen, his thumb brushed up against a foreign object, something—knobby. He grabbed hold of it, and recognized the shape of bead chain against his palm. Phillip yanked backward, bringing the chain with him.

The creature fell still.

It lowered its arm from Phillip's throat.

He fell back, gasping, to find his attacker staring at him, head tilted as if in curiosity. The flashlight lay on the ground a few feet away. The beam illuminated its ghastly face, but the menacing expression vanished.

"What *are* you?" Phillip repeated.

The creature clacked its teeth together, but did not speak or make any move to attack.

"I'm going to ... grab my flashlight."

It angled its head toward the light.

Phillip snatched up the light and pointed it directly at the thing that had been intent on killing him seconds before. It glanced down at its wounded arm and shook it. Then it looked back at Phillip.

"Can you understand me?"

It clacked its teeth together again, and Phillip took that as a *yes*.

"What the *hell*?" Phillip threw his arms up in bewilderment and exasperation, only then remembering the item clutched in his hand. He aimed the flashlight at it.

A dog tag. Just one, hanging on a bead-chain necklace.

"Holy shit."

Clack clack clack.

"Are you Corporal Alban Wren?"

The creature cocked its head, its eyes less milky than they'd been before, but still mostly vacant.

Then slowly, *Clack.*

"Holy shit."

Two hours later, Dr. Phillip Thorpe sat in a farmhouse the Order had rented as a safe house, just in case anything went wonky on the mission.

Well, it had. It had gone very wonky.

Alban sat in a chair across the table, staring at nothing in particular. Or maybe he wasn't staring. Phillip couldn't tell. But the guy hadn't moved in 30 minutes.

The Order Agents were supposed to arrive by private car sometime today, though Romanian train schedules were dicey. They hadn't been in contact. Phillip knew only that they were neophytes, but that Solan thought them competent enough to do reconnaissance work. Needless to say, they were not prepared for what they'd find when they got here. Animated corpses weren't exactly run-of-the-mill, even by Order standards, so these greenhorns were in for a shock.

"What do you think, Alban? Should I be nice and warn the junior Agents about you? Or let them be surprised?"

Clack clack.

"Well, I'm not sure what that means, but I'll take it under advisement."

The sun peeked over the mountains, and some of the folks at the dig site would be waking soon. Phillip called the foreman's number on his cell phone and left a voicemail that he had awakened early and was running into town for supplies. He'd think up something more thoroughly convincing later.

It was early afternoon when car tires crunched up the gravel driveway.

"Alright, Alban, buddy. I think I might be feeling like a nice guy today. Do you suppose you could come into this room for me so I can prepare the Agents to meet you?"

Alban stood and walked into the bathroom Phillip had motioned to, and Phillip pulled the door closed. Then he went to the window to see who the Order had sent.

The driver emerged first, then went and opened the two back doors to the vehicle before moving to the trunk. Two women got out of the car, both looking a bit road-weary and rumpled. One of them clutched a cup of coffee like a life line, and the other yawned and rubbed her eyes like a toddler.

"Are you kidding me?" he grumbled. "These aren't field Agents!"

They made their way up the walk, dragging their luggage over the loose stones. He whipped the door open before they got the chance to knock.

"You're in for more than you bargained for," he said by way of greeting.

"Well, good afternoon to you, too," the taller one said. The other one looked like she wanted to say something, but instead set her jaw and gave Phillip a steely glare. "I'm Esme, and this is my sister, *Dr.* Eliza Wren,"

Esme emphasized her sister's title, though Phillip couldn't tell if it was for clarification or a power move.

"Wren, huh?" he countered. "Boy, do I have a surprise for you."

"We already heard about our great-great uncle's dog tag," Esme informed him, adopting a tone of defiance at his less-than-polite welcome. "Do you suppose we might come inside?"

"Oh, certainly." He stepped aside, and his voice dripped with sarcasm. He couldn't quite figure out why, but he felt personally offended that the Order had sent what looked like a couple of sorority girls into the field for him to babysit. He needed *help*, and he didn't have time to hand-hold a couple of nepotism-babies whose surname had most likely gotten them rushed through training.

"Thanks," the shorter one rasped at him, pushing by him a little more forcefully than necessary.

Phillip knew he was being unprofessional and that he should be treating these women with every courtesy, but he was out of his depth with Alban, and he needed competent Agents to manage this situation.

"Look," he began, "I'm sorry for being a bit prickly. But we have a bit of a situation ..."

He never got to finish. A wail ripped from Esme's throat and her eyes rolled back in her head like she was about to have a seizure. Without warning, she launched herself at the closed bathroom door, falling to her knees and placing her palms against the wood. Sobs wracked her slender frame.

"No, no, noooo! Lost—despair—help!"

4

AN INTERVIEW WITH THE UNDEAD

Eliza caught Esme, a look of horror directed at their *host*. He was hiding something, and her sister sensed it. She wanted to scream at him, but at the moment, Esme screamed enough for both of them.

"Jeeze! What is wrong with her?" Dr. Thorpe had a look of horror painted on his slender face. His cheeks flamed red. He grabbed for his hair and took a step back, looking as if he might panic, too.

"Let me go! Let me go!" Esme cried out, fighting to escape Eliza's arms. Eliza loosened her grasp, but Esme didn't move. She seemed to bang the air with her fist in the same rhythm as the pounding on the door.

"What is that?" Eliza glanced back at the door, her voice gruff as she tried to speak more forcefully than she should. "Who's in there?"

Thorpe glared at her, his dark brown eyes calming as Esme's cries faded into a muttering plea to be set free. He threw up his hands then shoved them into his pockets. "You're not going to believe it."

"Show me," Eliza demanded, her voice cracking.

Thorpe shook his head and bit his lip like he didn't want to. Like he *wouldn't* do it. Eliza turned and started for the door. But the man bolted past her and blocked the way. "You're not going to believe it. It's ... it's ... *impossible.*"

Why, sometimes I've believed as many as six impossible things before breakfast, Eliza thought, but didn't have the strength to force the words aloud. "Show. Me." She punctuated each word, her body growing tense and her hands balling into fists.

Thorpe kept shaking his head, but he turned and went to the door. Eliza took a step back, wrapping her arms around her sister, as much to comfort herself as her sibling. The door opened, and Thorpe jumped back, pacing as he moved away from the hall, then came to stand in front of Eliza, blocking her view.

"You asked for this," he said, then stepped aside.

"Blimey!" Eliza recoiled when she saw it. Him. He was human, or had been. Scenes from **The Walking Dead**, an American television programme, flashed in her mind's eye. Her grip on Esme tightened as the thing shuffled towards them. He was a *dead man walking*, for certain. The smell of ancient decay lay heavy in the air. His clothing hung in rags on the near-skeletal frame. Eliza's hand went over her nose as she backed up with Esme again.

"Obey." Esme's voice hollowed and her muttering stopped. She seemed to come back to herself, her eyes burning red rather than cloudy gray. "Alban?"

"In the flesh," Thorpe said, blanching. "Pun intended."

Eliza let go of her sister and moved to study the being. He was certainly not among the living, but the term *zombie* didn't quite fit. "What ..." the words fell away even before they formed in her throat.

"At ease, soldier," Phillip said, and the corpse obeyed.

"*Reporting as ordered, sir.*" The words came from Esme's throat, but not in Esme's voice. The milky clouds appeared in her eyes again, as she stumbled toward the table and fell into a chair. Eliza moved to take the chair next to her, leaning in to inspect her. *I'll never get used to this,* she thought.

Phillip narrowed his eyes. "What's wrong with her?"

"Psychic," Eliza managed.

Phillip's brow reached for his receding hairline. He sank into the chair across from them. "She can communicate with the dead?"

Eliza's shoulder lifted, suggesting either that was the case or there might be more to it.

"What's wrong with *you*?" he snapped.

Taken aback, she locked eyes with him. It was a rude question, and she wasn't sure how to answer it, considering she *couldn't* answer it. Pursing her lips, she reached for the zipper on her jacket and pulled it down, unwrapping the scarf around her neck, exposing the razor-thin scar that flamed red on her neck. Short of wearing turtlenecks or a velvet ribbon around her neck for the rest of her life, there wasn't much she could do to hide it.

"Damn, girl! Who took a razor blade to you?"

"Long story," Eliza croaked.

After the initial shock wore off, the scientists came up with a plan. Phillip set the digital tape recorder in the middle of the table and tossed a notepad to Eliza. She took a pen from her shirt pocket and clicked it. Outside, the wind rattled the shutters, and the desolate farmhouse seemed colder for a moment. Phillip went and put another log on the fire before ordering Alban to take a seat.

The undead being complied, sitting stock-straight in his chair. Esme had a cup of tea in front of her and looked frightened by what was about to happen. Eliza reached a hand to her, offering silent comfort. She'd never force Esme to do anything she wasn't physically or mentally able to do, but this presented a rare and unique opportunity that most scientists never had the opportunity to achieve.

Eliza's gaze went to Alban—what was left of him. His eyes, dry and greyed, were unblinking, the pupils dilated. His lips hung away from his bony mouth, his front teeth pronounced and uneven. His jaw flexed and the *clack clack clack* echoed in the rafters overhead.

Phillip came back from the small kitchen with a cup of coffee that smelled sour and old. Eliza blanched but said nothing. Combined with the fetid odors already in the room, her stomach churned.

He reached out and flicked on the recorder. "Let's begin," he said. Phillip gave a protracted introduction to document the interview like a trained investigator. Date, time, location, names of those present, and details about the subject before them. "Found in a service tunnel beneath the South Wing, the *specimen* is mobile, partially desiccated, somewhat responsive to commands, and exhibits signs of sentience. Dog tags found on the subject identify him as Corporal Alban Wren of the British Army, declared missing and later killed in action in 1944. Testing a psychic interface via Miss Esme Wren."

He glanced at Eliza. "If you have any questions you want to ask, feel free to write them down and I'll ask them." The offer wasn't a kindness but a necessity. Her throat was especially sore, and she suspected all the testing and travel had done its worst. She unwrapped a lozenge, popping it in her mouth, then nodded and began scribbling questions.

Thorpe turned his attention to Esme, whose eyelids fluttered over cloudy eyes. "First question. For the record, state your name, rank, and serial number."

Esme's seemingly blind gaze went to the creature sitting at the end of the table. *Clack clack clack.*

"Wren, Alban. Corporal. 3rd Infantry, Royal Army Medical Corps, assigned to Field Unit K, special detachment." Esme spoke in the same voice she'd channeled before. She sounded like a young man, honored to serve, excited to see the world, but fearful of the perils of war. In truth, his thoughts were garbled and frenetic and she spent all her energy trying to translate the chaos.

Eliza scribbled notes on the page as he rattled off his serial number. She pushed her notepad over to Thorpe.

"What's your assignment here in Romania?" Thorpe read her question.

Clack, clack, clack.

"Support operations, sir," Esme answered.

Thorpe glanced over Eliza's notes as she scribed another question. "No. Your assignment for *the Order*," he repeated the question as written.

Clack, clack.

"Classified."

Phillip's eyes met Eliza's. The message that passed between them didn't need to be said. "Signal 42 Havana, Gallipoli, Tripoli, Gallipoli. Code name: Camouflage."

Eliza scribbled a note. Phillip's brow lifted. "We know about *Operation: Grimwell*."

Even the corpse seemed to stiffen; its jaw hung slack, eyeballs racing side to side before the jaw moved again. *Clack, clack, clack.*

Esme stiffened. "Identify and secure potentially lethal relics and cursed objects."

Phillip's brow lifted. "What happened beneath the hospital?"

Clack. Clack. Clack. Clack. Clack.

"They said it was a German top-secret initiative. A chance to test a relic ... one of the conscripted doctors from Spain carried it with him when they sent him to the front. I had been tracking this artifact on behalf of the Order. They called it the *Arkanos Artifact*."

Phillip turned to Eliza, whose eyes lit with recognition. "Have you heard of this relic?"

Eliza shook her head yes.

"We've heard of it, but what is the *Arkanos Artifact*?" Esme asked in her own voice.

"*The Healer's Shard*. A surgical blade. Roman."

Eliza scribbled furiously.

"Who was in charge of this project?"

"Dr. Escavarra. A well-reputed Spanish physician. But he changed. They called him ... *The Night Doctor*. He believed in restoration. He wanted to cure death. He said the Blade chose the worthy. Some survived. Some became malicious versions of themselves."

Eliza scratched an icon on her paper and pushed it to Phillip. The swastika gave him chills. He glanced up at Alban. "Did he work for the Nazis?"

Clack, clack. Clack.

"Conscripted, sir," Esme answered for the corpse. "Forced to work for them. They wanted an army. He wanted redemption. He said the pain was worth the price."

"Who was he using this blade on?"

Clack, clack.

"Prisoners," Esme blanched. Eliza's hair on her arms stood on end as the energy radiated from her sister. She envisioned the horrific prison camps and ghettos where prisoners of war were sent to die. She thought of Josef Mengele and his horrific experimentation on women, children, specifically twins. "Patients. Soldiers," Esme continued. "He cut us again and again..."

Mortui te exspectant, the voices in Eliza's head whispered.

Eliza's stomach churned and threatened revolt. She threw herself from the chair and raced out the door into the cold night. She fled to escape the horrors she saw in the back of her mind, not sure if the visions came from Esme or her own overactive imagination.

Phillip found her on her hands and knees, gasping for breath, fighting the urge to vomit. The cold air felt good on her hot cheeks. The icy winds provided the relief she needed, away from the odor of death and stale coffee.

"Are you okay?" Phillip asked.

Eliza sat back on her knees, feeling the damp soaking in through the fabric of her twill pants. Her eyes went to the night sky. A full moon hung low in the distance, casting a golden glow over the thin layer of snow that hung on the mountains to the north. Her breath came out like white clouds, hanging only for a moment around her face before the wind swept it away. She nodded. "Sorry," she gasped, choking on the word, coughing for a moment.

"No need to apologize to me," he said, reaching down to catch her and help her up. "But you'll freeze to death out here." He shivered as he forced her to her feet. "The sooner we get this done, the sooner it will all be over."

Eliza nodded and fell in beside him, returning to the house, brushing the mud from her knees. Esme sat at the table, sipping her tea as if nothing were amiss. "Are we done?"

"Not quite," Phillip said. "But your sister needed a break."

"Is the kettle still on? My tea's gone cold."

"Of course," Phillip took her cup and returned a moment later with a fresh cup, the tea bag still *in situ*. "Here you go."

Eliza noted the look of disdain on Esme's face as she took up the teabag and bounced it in the cup. Esme liked her tea a certain way, and didn't measure up to her standards. Loose leaf, jasmine, or oolong. On rare occasions, she might take peppermint or camomile, but they weren't her favorites. Lipton affronted her sensibilities. That was what they had, though, so she took it.

Eliza jotted down some additional notes while Esme calmly sipped the tea until she emptied the cup.

"Shall we continue?" Esme asked.

"When you're ready," Phillip said, tipping back his own cup.

Esme sat back in her chair and her lashes fluttered, her eyes going milky again.

"Soldier, tell us what happened to your unit," Phillip ordered.

Alban turned his head, directing his lifeless gaze from Esme to Phillip. *Clack, clack, clack. Clack, clack.*

"It was an ambush, sir," Esme said for him. "They pinned us in, then bombarded us with bullets and mortars. I took shrapnel to the chest and knew it was a fatal injury. The lads tried to help me, but ... I didn't last long. Bled out so fast. The bits probably nicked the aorta ..."

Eliza winced, but didn't bolt.

"He brought me back," Esme said, her lip trembling.

"Who?" Eliza managed.

"The Night Doctor ... the shard ... it brought me back, but not ...whole. I remember fire. Screaming ... my own. Then, silence."

"Are there others? Like you?" Phillip asked.

"Yes," Esme's voice conveyed the young man's emotions, but the look of sadness in the undead eyes struck the hardest. "Scattered. Buried. Some still wander. The Night Doctor sends them out to find more ... I hear him even now ..."

Eliza scribbled a note for Phillip.

"What does he want now?" Phillip asked for her.

Alban's gaze turned to Eliza. "You." Eliza gasped at Esme's pronouncement. "The Blade remembers you. It wants to finish what its brother began."

Esme stood, gasping for breath, then collapsed back in the chair, limp and unmoving. Phillip rushed to her aid, but Eliza froze, unable to move, unable to breathe, her gaze locked on the corpse of her great-great uncle.

Clack, clack, clack.

5

THE WEIGHT OF THE DEAD

The woods felt different.

Caspar Escaverra stared up at the massive building which had been his home for four decades, though not consecutively. He had tried to escape into the wider world, but his children were here, and they were his responsibility. The autumn wind rustled through the trees, black against the night sky, but something in their whispers was ... *off*. Even the crows who usually gathered in respectful vigil around the broken chimney were absent.

He stepped forward into the precarious-looking service entrance at the back of the hospital, a museum to old horrors and fragile hope. More people had suffered here than had been cured, he supposed. He owned some of that suffering, and the burden weighed on him.

His boots crunched over broken glass and withered leaves as he made his way through what had been a corridor for deliveries of medicines and equipment when the hospital had been filled with living souls, most of whom wanted to do good in the world, even if they didn't know how. Today it stood as a hollow shell filled with the hollow shells of men.

The air smelt of rotten vegetation and dust. That much was familiar. But the air lacked the resonance he'd come to associate with his *Awakened sons*. The hum of the relic in his coat pocket had been insistent on his expedited return from Bucharest, and now his own senses vibrated with a thrum of wrongness. The rhythm of undead stillness felt off-kilter. Esteban's presence always brushed against his consciousness when he was here. Alban and the others less so, but even they left a trace.

Tonight, the hum was diminished somehow.

Caspar's pulse quickened as he descended into the basement tunnel, guided more by memory than by light. The entrance to the fallout shelter lay hidden behind the rusty supply locker. He shifted it aside with practiced ease and unlocked the steel hatch beneath.

The old air met him like a sigh.

He descended the narrow metal stairs into the main chamber and found the switch. The dim lights—jury-rigged from scavenged bits and bobs of generators left behind—still worked. One flickered overhead as he entered the chamber he referred to as the Crucible.

Aluminum autopsy tables and gurneys where his sons would "sleep" when they weren't active—which was most of the time—edged with aluminum edged the perimeter of the room. Eight of the nine makeshift beds were now occupied. All accounted for except Alban, who would be guarding the tunnel exit that led to a different part of the hospital's basement. The relic, which the Covenant had referred to as the *Artifact of Arkanos*—oh, they did love their dramatic titles—thrummed in his pocket, amplifying his sense of unease.

Caspar made his way to the hatch that led into the tunnel he'd left Alban to patrol. He walked it end to end.

Empty. His heart thumped against his ribs. What did this mean?

He returned to the Crucible, stopping only for a moment to look upon Esteban, who lay in his long, deathless torpor. Then he crossed to his desk and opened the oblong metal box and retrieved the crude tracking talismans he had fashioned from a ritual of bone, thread, and blood. Each was calibrated to one of his Awakened sons' energies.

He sifted through the box: Antonio, Francisco, Manuel—all intact. But the fourth one—Alban's—was shattered. A spiderweb of cracks across the talisman's glass face glinted in the weak light.

"No ..." He stood in the center of the shelter, slowly turning, listening. The silence now tasted like judgement.

Caspar held the fractured talisman in his left hand as he produced the Artifact from his breast pocket with his right. The blade responded, flashing as if in recognition. But the whispers that usually came from it were unclear. Disrupted.

Alban was gone. Taken ... or worse. His hands trembled as he tried to work the clasp on his bag. For 80 years, he'd managed to keep them hidden, and now one of his Awakened was missing.

He grabbed his journal from his valise, flipping through the pages with shaking hands until he found his notes about Alban's Turning and subsequent ritual experiments. Failed resurrection sigils, momentary signs of re-sentience ... after decades of research, he was so close; he just knew it.

But if Alban was out in the world, he couldn't bear to think about what would happen. Had his British soldier-son been captured? All Caspar's work would come crumbling down, and none of his sons were safe.

"Ez, can I get you anything?" Eliza poked her head into the darkened room where Esme lay sprawled on the bed, rubbing her temples and moaning in pain.

"Do you have about 50 Nurofen I could take? Because my head's been through a grinder."

"Here, sit up." Eliza knelt on the bed behind her sister, rubbing the spot in her neck that sometimes got knotted up when Esme had overwhelming visions. "Your muscles feel like they're packed with golf balls." She kept her voice to a whisper in order to be gentle on her sore vocal chords.

"That sounds about right. I've never experienced anything like that, Eliza. It's like he used part of *my* mind to make sense of the jumbled-up images in *his*."

"I thought you were channeling his spirit, like when Eleanor occupied my body and spoke through me." Eliza shuddered at the memory.

"No, this wasn't like that. Uncle Alban isn't a ghost. He's corporeal. But his brain's mostly mothballs at this point, so he can't really form clear thoughts. I'm an empath, so my mind reached out to his, and then his sort of climbed back through the connection. That's the best way I can think to explain it. I loaned him my ability to think, and once his mind figured out what was happening, he used me like a Bluetooth speaker."

"Is that why he got quiet and still again when you came upstairs?"

Esme nodded. "I'm a little too far for him to reach now, so he's back in *standby mode*."

"He could hurt you."

"I wasn't prepared for it. He won't be able to dig in so hard again. But he's been so alone for so long, Liza. I could feel it. Until Dr. Thorpe yanked that tag out of Uncle Alban's side, the poor man was ... stuck. He didn't have any free will at all. I don't want him to feel abandoned if I'm the only one who can speak for him. Besides, he might know more about the Night Doctor."

"Do you really think so?"

"Maybe. He didn't seem to know much about what happened after he ... died, I guess. That part felt fuzzy."

"Speaking of fuzzy, put your pajamas on and I'll find you some Nurofen. Maybe you'll feel better after some sleep."

"Lord, I hope so. Uncle Alban cracked my brain like an egg."

Philip sat on the threadbare sofa staring at Alban, who sat stiff and upright in the wing chair in the corner. Dr. Thorpe, Order Agent and archaeologist, fancied himself a bit of an Indiana Jones type, walking the line between magic and history, but he'd never seen anything like this. The whole operation was far bigger than anyone could have known.

And now he found himself with trainees at his disposal instead of seasoned Agents. The Grand Aegis's judgement was usually sound, but his fondness for the Wren family might just get Phillip killed.

The farmhouse kitchen creaked with every gust of wind that blew through the aged shutters. The musty odor of disuse clung to everything. Couldn't the Order have sprung for a housekeeper to spruce the place up?

Upstairs, Esme slept fitfully. She hadn't stirred since collapsing on the guest bed after taking the headache tabs. She'd pushed herself too far, and was likely to do it again.

Eliza paced between the parlor and the kitchen, exhausted, but filled with nervous energy.

In the corner, Alban sat in his chair like a puppet with his strings cut. Without Esme, he sat dormant, less a person than a corpse or an automaton waiting for orders.

"Stop pacing," Phillip muttered from the sofa, hunched over a coffee table littered with notes and dusty books. "You're making it harder to think."

Eliza stopped but didn't think. "Good," she rasped. "Thinking ... hasn't done ... much good ... so far."

Phillip looked up sharply. "Excuse me?"

Eliza laid her hand across her neck as if she could give her throat support as it spilled all of her frustrations. "We're sitting in a ... crumbling farmhouse ... with a reanimated war casualty ... from 1944 propped up ... in a comfy chair." Eliza paused, swallowing hard. "My sister's upstairs ... with a headache that ... might qualify as a minor stroke, and ... the only other Aegis Field Agent ... is what? Preparing a ... book report?" She winced. It was the most she'd said at one time since Maelis had slit her throat.

His jaw tightened. "I've been in the field with the Order for 15 years. This isn't my first entity of questionable origin."

"No, but ... is it your first family member?" she snapped, gesturing to Alban. "Because he's my blood. Esme's too. That connection ... is why we're here."

"I'm aware of the lineage," Phillip said coolly, "but this isn't an initiation trial. This is classified relic interference in the natural order, a decades-old resurrection ritual with possible Nazi connections, and an undead soldier with unknown intent. It's not a campfire story. It's a threat."

Eliza stared at him, her eyes burning. "We didn't ask to be here. We were sent. And you think we're underqualified? Esme is the ... only reason he's been able to ... communicate. Without her, you'd be documenting... muscle twitches ... and guessing at ... war trauma."

Phillip hesitated, walking the line between irritation and fatigue. This woman exhausted him. "Look, I'm not trying to belittle either of you. But this is spiraling fast. You heard him. This isn't a random resurrection. This has the marks of the Covenant. And if they're involved ..."

"Then we don't have time ... to wait for backup," Eliza finished, softening. "We don't need ... to be battle-ready. We need to be ... *here*."

They stared at each other in tense silence, the only sound was the *tick-tick-tick*ing of the old clock on the wall, followed by a *clack clack* from Alban.

Then Phillip sighed, leaned back from the cluttered table and motioned for her to sit. "Alright, we need to prioritize. First: containment. If this Night Doctor guy is still active, he'll come looking for Alban, and he probably won't be alone. And given how old he'd have to be, we should probably assume that whatever the Artifact did to Alban, it's somehow extending the Doctor's life, too. Second: location. We need to find his base of operations where he's doing his experiments or rituals or whatever. Third ..."

"... we need to ... protect Esme. If the *Arkanos Artifact* is ... connected to Alban, it might know *his* blood."

"He did say it knew you. That it was coming for you."

Eliza crossed her arms, tension rolling off her like heat. But she nodded. She needed some of that Nurofen herself. Even whispering hurt if she did enough of it.

"Then we rest tonight and take turns on watch. Tomorrow, we get to work."

6

Hic Iacent Mortui

"Solan, what are you trying to do to me?" Phillip snarled, keeping his voice low.

"You're a *senior* field Agent," Solan retorted. He wasn't happy about being called away from his morning repast, nor the reason for the call. "The job of any Agent is to foster new Field Agents. Training is something you are good at or I wouldn't have sent them to work with you."

"You only sent them because they are Simon Wren's daughters."

"You forget yourself, Dr. Thorpe," Solan snapped. "While I am Grand Aegis, I will not have my decisions questioned. Eliza and Esme are best suited for the task. You will need them and they will need you."

"Solan?" Eliza croaked, coming down the stairs to join Phillip at the table. The argument had awakened her, but she was still bleary-eyed and groggy. "What's wrong?"

"Dr. Thorpe has informed me about the sudden change to your mission," Solan said. "He has concerns about your safety considering what ... ah ... considering what Esme channeled from your ... *ancestor* in regards to the Blade's sentience and its threat to you." He hemmed and hawed, not sure how to answer. "I assured him that your health is sound, and you and your sister have all the skills necessary to accomplish the mission."

"So ..." Eliza coughed, clearing her voice. "What's our mission now?"

"You will need to investigate. Collect data. Find out about this Night Doctor, and if possible, locate the *Artifact of Arkanos*, if it's even there. You will need to secure it and return it to Aegis HQ with utmost haste. But be warned. If the Covenant is also looking for it, you can trust no one."

"So what do we do with Uncle Alban?" Esme said, appearing at the base of the stairs.

"He will need to be returned to Aegis HQ as well, but we'll cross that bridge when we get there," Solan said. "Report back once you've completed your initial reconnoiter."

"Aye, aye, Captain," Esme said, saluting. Eliza shot a stern glare at her sister.

"We'll discuss my other concerns later, Solan." Phillip scowled.

"No, we won't," Solan said. "My decision is final." The line went dead.

"What other concerns?" Esme asked.

"Nothing," Phillip ran a weary hand down his face. "It's something to do with a previous case."

Nice cover, Eliza thought. She didn't believe it for a second.

"What's for breakfast?" Esme asked, stifling a yawn.

"I'm not your chef," Phillip said. "Help yourself to whatever you can find. I need a shower."

"I'll make tea," Eliza grumped.

Esme rifled through the cupboards looking for something to eat. They'd gotten to work straight away upon arrival the night before, and she hadn't had anything since the layover in Vienna. They'd hoped to grab something after landing at the Sibiu International Airport. However, their flight had been delayed. They arrived much later than either had planned, and they still had an almost two-hour drive to get to the remote location near Zlatna. To say she was hungry was an understatement. Esme's stomach growling as Eliza put the kettle on.

"This is a bachelor's kitchen if ever I saw one," Esme groused. "Did we pass a market on our way in?"

"Who knows," Eliza croaked. "So dark."

"Yeah, it was dark," Esme agreed. "I'm not sure I've ever been somewhere as dark as it is here at night."

"No light pollution." Eliza's gaze went toward the window. Dawn had broken, but the sky above the trees glowed pale pink.

Eliza went to the refrigerator for milk. What she found was disappointing. The carton of milk was almost empty. She opened it to look inside, and caught a green glow off the contents. The sour smell that arose from the carton immediately turned her stomach and she felt green herself. The sound revulsion came from her throat and she closed the carton and held it away from her face as far as her arm would allow. *Sweet Jesus*, she muttered in her head.

"I take it the milk's gone off?" Esme asked, taking the carton away, tossing it in the refuse bin.

Eliza nodded, trying to clear her memory of that odor. "No lemon either."

Esme went to the fridge and gazed in, repugnant indignation blooming in her features as she pulled out cartons of old Chinese food, spoiled lunch meat and mouldy cheese. "We're going to have to find a market."

"Drink your tea," Eliza said, pointing to the cup with the teabag. "I'll get dressed. Work first."

"Maybe there's a Starbuck's somewhere?"

The thought of Phillip's stale coffee came back to her and Eliza couldn't get upstairs fast enough.

Alban stood at attention in the living area of the cabin, while Phillip barked orders at him. "You are to remain at your post, on guard, at all times."

"Oh, come now," Eliza questioned his orders. "Make him stand all day?"

Phillip glared at her, his lips pursed and his brown eyes filled with irritation. "I am his commanding officer."

"Sounds like Solan."

Whether it was Eliza's words or the very fact that she threw Solan's orders in his face, she couldn't be sure, but Phillip didn't seem to like the comparison.

"Belay that," Phillip barked. "Sit in that chair." He pointed at a wicker chair in the corner, out of the way, tucked behind a bookcase with half a dozen old novels written in some foreign language Eliza didn't understand. She'd come down in the night looking for something to read, only to find the books were useless to her.

Alban tottered over to the chair, his body moving in a way that a human form shouldn't move. Whether caused by the desiccated muscle or lack of free will, Eliza couldn't be certain. When he bumped into the chair, his teeth chattered and he took small steps, turning. While the journey to the chair was protracted, his collapse into the seat was not. One second he stood, the next, he sat. *Clack, clack, clack.*

"Do not move from that spot until I give the order," Phillip said.

"Sit. Stay." Eliza cast a wicked stare at Phillip as she patted Alban on the shoulder. "Good boy, Alban."

"So, where are we going?" Esme asked from the backseat of Phillip's SUV, a *Škoda Kodiaq* that had seen better days. The paint peeled away, and oxidized in places where it'd sat in the sun. The interior appeared no better. Leaf litter, pine needles, rocks and the occasional French fry lay in the crevices and were embedded in the carpet. It carried the pungent scent of mould and stale cigarettes that suggested it had been smoked in, though not recently.

"We'll start at the dig site," he said. "I'll let the senior archaeologist show you where we found *the artifacts*. Dr. Lázár, he's the only one who knows *what* I found, by the way."

Eliza was certain he meant Alban's service tag ... and Alban himself. She studied the archaeologist as he drove the mountainous roads, the switchbacks making her nauseous with each turn of the wheel.

He didn't look like a smoker. No wrinkles in the creases of his upper lip, though beneath what might have been a week's worth of stubble. His skin was pale, except for the flares of cold in his cheeks and the tip of his long, hooked nose. He had dark circles around his jet eyes that cut into the laugh lines around them.

He was older than Eliza by at least ten years, if she had to wager a guess. American. Arrogant. Stubborn. She'd known several Thorpes in her life, though all the others were of British descent. One of her college advisors had been a delightful old girl from Suffolk, Jane Thorpe-Goodall. She'd guided Eliza into engineering when she hadn't been quite sure which path to take, and Eliza never regretted it. In her graduation speech, she'd mentioned her by name, thankful for her guidance. The words ran through her mind as she closed her eyes and tried to still her stomach.

Before I go any further, I would like to thank someone whose quiet encouragement and steady belief in me made all the difference: Mrs. Jane Thorpe-Goodale, your kindness remained a constant in the chaos of my early academic years. Your gentle nudges, always perfectly timed, helped steer me back on course more than once. You never pushed too hard, but you always knew when I needed a word of encouragement, a spark of confidence or a reminder that I was worthy of every accolade and accomplishment that I'd worked for. I wouldn't be standing here today without your guidance and I am so deeply and truly grateful. May we all have such strong mentors in our lives.

Mentors were important. If this man weren't so bloody full of himself, he might be an excellent one. She'd looked up his background on the way to the airport and had been impressed with his academic credentials. The polymath's accolades were every bit equal to her own, though divergent.

He graduated *Summa Cum Laude* from the University of Chicago with a dual bachelor's degree in linguistics and pre-med, a masters in both philosophy and history. His honors thesis had been a study of 19th-century mass grave sites across Eastern Europe. He went on to study at Johns Hopkins University School of Medicine and Department of Anthropology, obtaining a dual PhD/MD. She couldn't deny his brilliance. His multiple degrees were proof of it.

Eliza found his PhD dissertation in a publication online and read it word for word. *Trauma Medicine and the Myth of the Untouchable Healer: The Rise of Medical Exceptionalism in the 20th Century.* It was a beautifully-written paper, novel-worthy had it not been a technical examination of outliers in the medical community. He called out everyone from Josef Mengele to Dr. Phil. Questioning their motives. Challenging their ethics. Villainizing their practices. Cutting to the bone with his sharp wit and clever turn of phrase. While academia lauded the dissertation for its insight and depth, it also earned him a reputation as a contrarian in medical, archaeological and anthropological circles.

She'd also scanned through the Aegis database for information on him ... as a person *and* an Agent. Within the Order, Dr. Phillip Thorpe was regarded as both an asset and an anomaly. With the knowledge and skill of both a physician and an archeologist/anthropologist, not to mention the vocabulary of a philosopher and linguist, the Order recruited Thorpe not for his belief in the arcane, but his constant ability to analyze and survive it.

His first mission, over ten years before, had been in Northern Syria where the accidental unsealing of a Bronze Age plague reliquary nearly unleashed a pandemic worse than the Black Death itself. Thorpe quarantined the entire camp and began treating the infected with little in the way of resources, by torchlight. When help arrived, the contagion had been contained, the ill were stabilized, and he'd already begun working to isolate the virus with a *Dynamo-Lite AM1199* handheld digital microscope, purifying, counting and characterizing the virus.

Thorpe's reputation spoke to his ethos and expertise, his sharp tongue and an aversion to hypocrisy—not to mention bureaucracy— often placed him at odds with command. Whether the Grand Aegis trusted him or not, if Eliza were bleeding out in a cursed underground sanctuary or abandoned mental hospital, she'd want him there. She made a silent vow to try and win him over as an ally. They would need to work together in order to accomplish their objective. There was no time for petty dissent.

Still, the scowl etched into his features now suggested he was not happy. She knew why. He didn't know them from Adam or Eve, and in reality they *were* rookies. But Eliza and Esme weren't untested. They'd taken down the High Seer of the Covenant and beheaded the organization in the doing of it. Of course, it hadn't been without a price. If she'd learned anything from their first experiences in the field, it was that *there was always a price*. It cost her a life, and her voice.

The tunnel stank of mouldering earth and something older. An iron-rich tang clung to the back of Eliza's throat. Just beyond the collapsed main corridor of the old asylum, a team of archeologists dug a trench into the rubble, exposing layers of forgotten architecture.

The original foundations of the hospital, laid in the late 1800s, had crumbled into warped catacombs, drainage channels that twisted downward into darker undocumented wings. Crumbling bricks gave way to bone-white mortar and soot-streaked tile, as if the very walls of the ancient structure had absorbed the residue of anguish and suffering.

Work lights cast sharp shadows on the faces of those bent over their work in the bottom of the trench as they gazed up at the approaching Agents. Eliza studied the crumbling walls that arched over their heads, water dripping from the cracks. Someone had scrawled crude symbols on a collapsing support beam. It was probably spray paint, but it too had oxidized and looked more like dried blood.

The thought sent shivers down Eliza's spine. Esme, noticing her sister's distraction, lifted the torch to illuminate the markings. Cyrillic lettering harkened back to her memories of **The Walking Dead** again. A padlocked door with a cautionary warning. *Don't Open. Dead Inside.* That might not have been precisely what it said, but that's what came to mind.

"Dr. Wren?" She turned and realized the lead archeologist had climbed up out of the excavation, wiping his hands on the seat of his pants, then the front of his shirt before sticking it out to her. "Pleasure to meet you."

Eliza fumbled, not sure what she'd missed. She recovered and took his hand, shaking it. "Pleasure," she said. "I'm sorry. Missed your name."

"I'm Dr. Gregor Lázár." He smiled brightly. "Welcome." He turned and waved a hand toward the excavation. He looked like a man carved out of the Carpathians themselves. His back folded like mountains of his homeland.

A well-groomed beard framed his face. His eyes were deep-set, eyes that had seen far too much history unearthed with far too little ceremony. He dropped his voice. "Welcome to my little corner of Hell. May I offer you coffee? I have a thermos in my field office."

"No," Eliza said, perhaps a bit too quickly. "Thank you."

"The Wrens have asked me to give them an overview of your findings and would like to see the location so they have a better feel for what we're dealing with." Phillip saved them from unnecessary pleasantries.

Dr. Lázár's smile seemed to fade as he nodded. "I've spent decades studying the fractured anatomy of old Europe. I've explored tunnels carved by monks and madmen. Burial vaults used by plague doctors. Monasteries that were built on bones older than the Scriptures. I've always approached history with a kind of reverence, like a physician diagnosing an unhealing wound in the earth. This hospital was built over the crumbled foundation of an earlier structure, possibly a former monastery or plague crypt. Not likely a hospital, based on what we've found."

Eliza squatted down at the edge of the excavation, careful not to tumble head-first into the void, but curious to observe the process. Esme knelt beside her, scanning the dig with similar curiosity. "What have you found?" Esme asked. "Besides ..." She let her word trail off then clacked her teeth to mimic Alban. *Clack, clack, clack.*

Dr. Lázár seemed to recoil at the thought. Recovering, he curled a finger towards the girls, indicating they should follow. "The architecture in the tunnels, which were probably part of the previous structure, are consistent with a monastery or crypt. Observe the carved stone archways and columns. We've found these crypt-like chambers." He pointed to a partially-excavated void where the walls had come in over the centuries. "There are small niches and alcoves where skeletal remains and burial urns have been found. We're awaiting radio carbon dating on the bones, but earlier testing of other artifacts suggest the structures to be medieval, if not older. There have been fragments of chalices, crosses engraved with obscure symbols worn by those buried here, beads that suggest ancient rosaries, and pottery sherds."

Eliza's gaze went up again as they neared a stone wall at the back of the tunnel, 90 metres, if her assessment was accurate, from the excavation. Over the arched wall, an ancient inscription was barely legible. She couldn't be certain, but thought it might say *Hic iacent mortui*.

Phillip leaned in and lowered his tone. "Do you read Latin, Dr. Wren?"

"A little" Eliza said. She didn't want to admit that she had little more than a textbook knowledge of the language.

"Can you make it out?" he asked.

A cold gust of wind found its way under her collar and through her scarf, as she studied the words again. She could almost hear the faint moans like ancient prayers, and the tapping of bones against one another as she translated, *"Here lie the dead."*

7

WHAT THE DARKNESS HIDES, THE LIGHT REVEALS

The rising sun crested the hills east of Zlatna, turning the sky from a bruised violet-grey to a pale pink as Caspar Escaverra pushed through the brush, one hand gripping Esteban's shoulder as they skirted the incline above the mine shaft.

His son—both by blood and by magic—moved stiffly, his pale skin catching the morning sun like wax. His eyes were hollow, blinking slowly and too rarely, but he followed Caspar's orders. He had no choice. None of them did, once a personal object of theirs was embedded within their bodies. Without such a token, the Awakened were uncontrollable, exaggerated undead versions of whatever primary characteristic they had embodied in life.

Esteban had become rebellious, chaotic, even violent when Caspar had spotted the outline of the ring in his abdomen and tried to remove it. When he returned it to the boy's body cavity, which had required that Esteban be restrained by a number of Nazi guards, his son had returned to this state of compliance. Less trouble, certainly, but empty of anything resembling a soul.

Caspar muttered half-formed prayers as he knelt beside the shaft, brushing aside stones and dirt. He pried the rickety old gate open. The shaft still held: dry, deep, sheltered. A reasonable place to hide the Awakened until the rituals could resume.

But Esteban faltered.

The undead boy staggered as they crossed the streambed. Even the weak sunlight seemed to hang on him like chains. Other than Alban, Esteban was the strongest of them, but the passage through the woods had been difficult for him. They could not evacuate the others and cross in daylight. The progress would be too slow.

Caspar's panic sharpened. He had hoped the curse's influence would wane in the light, not intensify. Only in darkness would they be able to make the journey. But with Alban missing, an element of urgency loomed. The real danger was time.

They returned to the sanatorium just after mid-morning. The hospital crouched in the clearing, a desecrated tomb. It should have been as dead as the things sleeping beneath it.

But something was wrong.

Voices.

He pulled Esteban down beside him and dropped to a crouch behind a ragged bush, peering through the thicket.

Beyond the cracked and overgrown courtyard, a bright splash of orange caught his eye: a nylon tent. Surveying equipment lay scattered about, and a white tarpaulin fluttered in the breeze. Students and laborers moved like ants over what had been the back lawn—digging, cataloguing, and brushing stone with absurd care.

He narrowed his eyes.

They weren't just on the grounds ... they were excavating the foundation ruins. And beneath that, they'd find ...

Caspar's stomach turned. *The abbey.* The old Roman-Christian crossover site. He suspected something even older lay beneath. Maybe that's why the Covenant had picked this location for him as a base for his research. Why the Blade had resonated here.

But now these outsiders were digging.

They had no idea what they might uncover. Worse—they were between him and his sons.

Caspar pressed himself and Esteban deeper into the foliage as a student crossed too close to the tunnel that had provided access to the hospital's basement and the fallout shelter before it had collapsed after the earthquake. If they excavated that ... if they stumbled on the fallout shelter ... if they found the Awakened ... they'd panic. They might call the authorities or worse ... someone from the Covenant might be embedded within their group.

His one solace was that it seemed to be business-as-usual now, which probably meant that they didn't know about Alban.

He pulled back, inch by inch, until he and Esteban were deep enough in the trees to vanish.

They had to creep along the concrete wall that had once partitioned off a staff area. Then they snuck into the hospital's basement, and it had taken hours to do so undetected. They had descended carefully into the shelter just before noon, hunched and sweating despite the autumn breeze.

Esteban had returned to his slab, inert.

The others, seven in total, lay on their gurneys as well. A soldier, a nurse, two locals, and three Jews who the Nazis had not been able to destroy before the Covenant helped him escape. He had refused to leave them behind. He wasn't a monster, after all.

They were his burdens, his failures, his hope for redemption.

He paced the chamber muttering words in Latin and broken Greek, fragments of prayers meant for Aesculapius, god of medicine, but laced with older invocations.

"Dis Pater ... Mors invicta ... Accepta placatio ..."

He paused at his journal, flipping to a drawing of the Plutonian Gate at Baiae, annotated with wild, ink-spattered speculation. Pluto had not been worshipped, only placated. His cults rites were esoteric and cloaked in shadows.

And that secrecy had birthed the Blade's curse.

Only by understanding the ritual that bound the Blade to Pluto's dominion could Caspar hope to unbind it. It was the only way to undo the broken resurrection and the only way to give Esteban and the *others* back their souls.

But now the outside world was closing in.

He had until nightfall to prepare. After that, he would need to move the Awakened in quiet and darkness. If they were discovered ...

No.

They would not be.

He would protect his sons.

Even if it meant killing again.

The sounds of trowels and brushes faded behind her as Esme stepped away from the dig site and into the overgrown area that used to be the hospital lawn. The leaves whispered like they were trying to warn her, but she didn't listen.

She didn't *mean* to wander. She just did.

The vines clinging to the hospital's west side curled like fingers, half-heartedly pulling at her coat as she stepped through the arch of what had once been the sanatorium's main entrance. The wooden doors had partially rotted away, giving the impression of jagged teeth in an open mouth. She paused just inside the threshold, catching her breath.

The lobby lay before her like the remains of a stage after the performance of a tragedy: torn curtains, shattered floor tiles, and a skeletal reception desk tipped on its side. Rain-stained paint peeled in ribbons away from the walls and the uncertain light filtered through the cracked windows.

But Esme didn't see any of that.

She saw shadows. She heard echoes.

They weren't voices exactly, but impressions like the murmur of old conversations still reverberating off the stone decades after all the people had left. The words weren't in English, but the thought behind them translated into Esme's head like whispered subtitles.

You're going to be fine. You just need to rest.

We need more quinine on the second floor.

I told you, stay out of the basement!

The air felt thick with memory. She closed her eyes. She could feel the hospital's *soul*, if such a thing existed. It was fragmented, bitter, held together by grief and crumbling concrete. It had seen too much. It was tired.

And beneath that exhaustion, she caught something else. Something recent.

A static buzzed in her chest, just under her ribs. It wasn't fear. It wasn't pain. But it was garbled, like a radio tuned to a station that shouldn't exist.

Her head throbbed. Her fingertips tingled.

She pressed her hand to the wall—mildew-streaked and cold—and the static spiked. Faces flickered behind her eyelids that were not fully human.

Not anymore. Their eyes were sunken, their skin waxy, like Alban's. But their expressions were locked somewhere between sorrow and obedience.

They were not ghosts or spirits. They were bound ... controlled. Something anchored them deep within. They were what Alban must have been before Dr. Thorpe had pulled the identification tag out of his desiccated gut.

"Esme!"

She snapped her eyes open. The static didn't vanish, it just stepped back.

Eliza's strained voice echoed from the doorway, her boots crunching on the glass.

Esme turned, stepping away from the wall just as her sister appeared, half-worried, half-annoyed. "What the bloody hell ..."

Esme opened her mouth, then closed it. She didn't know what to say. How could she explain the weight of the air or the *wrongness* humming under the skin of the building?

"It needed someone to notice," she breathed. "But it didn't want help. It's just watching."

Eliza pressed her lips together, too tired to try and decode Esme's oblique explanation. Her eyes scanned the broken windows and collapsed doorframes. "Come on then. This place is a ... tetanus buffet. Let's go."

Esme hesitated, casting one last long look at the wall. At the air. At the invisible pulse she couldn't unfeel. "They're not gone," she said, mostly to herself. "They're waiting. The Blade is here, too. Just like Uncle Alban said."

Eliza gently took her arm and led her back into the sunlight.

8

VINEGAR AND REGRET

Phillip found Eliza sitting on the half-wall in front of the main entrance of the abandoned asylum. Her thousand-yard stare told him she wasn't in a good place. Not mentally. He'd already run into Esme who simply said, "I'm starving," as she stormed past him, headed toward the car.

He couldn't argue with that. The cup of coffee he'd had this morning had turned to dust in his gullet and churned at odds with his guts. The nearest restaurant was a good twenty minutes away, but he knew there was nothing in the kitchen back at the farm house and they couldn't keep going like this.

"Dr. Wren?" he said again. She flinched when she realized he was standing in front of her. "Are you okay?" Her gaze went to her hands, folded tightly in her lap. "Eliza?"

She didn't answer. She didn't look up. She wrung her hands in a way that reminded him of Lady Macbeth, tormented in guilt after the murder of King Duncan in the famous Shakespearean play that no one in the theatre dare mention.

"That which hath made them drunk hath made me bold," Phillip quoted.

Eliza looked up at him blankly. "Alack, I am afraid they have awaked."

"Methought I heard a voice cry, *Sleep no more! Macbeth does murder sleep ... the innocent sleep ...*"

Eliza's gaze went long again and she heaved a heavy sigh. "Still it cried, *Sleep no more! to all the house. Macbeth shall ... sleep no more.*" She spoke with a voice that faded mid-sentence and lacked forte and fortitude.

"You know your Shakespeare," he acknowledged with a nod.

"Only ... the tragedies," she managed. "I'm afraid I'm not fond of his comedies, nor the sonnets."

Phillip bit his lip, narrowed his brow and considered her for a long moment. Sorrow seeped from her soul—unlike anyone he'd ever met. Beautiful in a simple way, but with no joy in her countenance. The dark circles beneath her lashes suggested that perhaps once there had been a light in those green eyes, but no longer. He let out a long sigh before dusting off the rock beside her. He took a seat on it. "Let me guess," he said. "You're cataloguing everything that's gone to hell here. Dead men walking around, cursed blades, mad scientists, crumbling ruins ..."

"A madman playing God ..." Her voice cracked and sounded even more gravelly than it had. "Poor Uncle Alban."

"You're not used to field work; I get it," Phillip allowed. "The harder it gets, the closer you are to success. Don't give up yet."

"Don't try to psychoanalyze me." Eliza stood, moving stiffly. "You don't know me."

He lifted a brow and shook his head, doing everything but laughing at her response. "Dr. Wren, I've been doing this for over a decade. I've seen rookies in the field buckle under less pressure."

"I'm not ... a rookie," she coughed mid-sentence. "Worked for Aegis for six years."

"But this is your first field assignment, right?" He leaned in. "I've seen it a dozen times. Brilliant types trying to outrun their own humanity. You think you can just sashay in here and solve the mystery right off the bat. You're not invincible. Just because you're a Wren doesn't mean this is going to come naturally."

"Is this your ... idea of compassion? Or just an excuse to ... lecture me?"

Thorpe recoiled at the harshness of her tone before he answered. "A bit from column A, but don't think I won't lecture you. I'm here to train you and I cannot fill a cup that is already full. Are you teachable, Dr. Wren? Or do you have it all figured out?"

Eliza tensed. She looked away again. Her breath caught. It wasn't a sob, just the hint of one that didn't make it out.

"Esme isn't ... okay." She forced the words. "I know my sister."

Phillip considered her for a moment, realizing it wasn't her own ego, but concern for Esme, that had built the wall around her. "Something ... I can't fix. Can't protect her from."

"Good thing I'm here," Phillip said, standing and taking a step towards her.

Eliza took a step back, keeping the distance between them like an invisible shield. "Alban ... shouldn't be. Shouldn't ... *exist*. I ... don't know how ... to help him either."

She looked up at him, her eyes rimmed in red, her pupils dark as a sun-dappled pool in a hidden wood. Those eyes, my God, he could drown in them and die a happy man. His heart broke for her. "Here's the thing, Wren," he said, trying to break through this spell she'd cast over him. "You don't have to stop it. You're just here to understand it. That's the job. And I know it sucks. But you're not alone in it."

She blinked slowly and he realized the space between them had melted away. He stood with her upper arms in his hands, their faces dangerously close to one another. He could smell the floral shampoo from her hair. Her breath was warm on his skin. "You're not a machine." She nodded. "Now, let's go find something to eat before I quote the Hippocratic Oath, or some such nonsense."

Eliza seemed to have escaped the moment of melancholy. "You'd probably ... quote the wrong one," she spoke weakly.

"There's more than one?" Phillip's brow shot up.

"Well, there's the classic one ... the botched version ... involving leeches and bloodletting ..."

"Why don't you explain it in the car on our way to town," he said.

Phillip had no idea there were three versions of the Hippocratic Oath or that the more modern version, known as the *Declaration of Geneva,* had been created by the World Medical Association after World War II in response to the medical atrocities of doctors like this so-called Night Doctor. An even more modern version, known as the *Lasagna version,* after Dr. Louis Lasagna removed references to God and focused more on patient autonomy, empathy and lifelong learning.

By the time they got to town, the only thing he could think of was lasagna and maybe some nice crusty French bread and a glass of red wine. The only restaurant open in town, however, offered no such fare.

Of course, by that point, Phillip didn't care.

The bistro was small, low-ceilinged, and warm, with the aroma of woodsmoke, roasting meat and something pickled. Mismatched tablecloths covered crooked tables. Folk music played on a boombox in the corner behind the counter, where a grandmotherly woman sat behind the cash register.

It reminded Eliza of a little cafe close to Oxford. She often went there when she needed a cuppa and a scone. It was a quiet, out of the way place where she could read a book and decompress after a long day of classes. Something smelled wonderful and her mouth watered. The waitress seated them in the corner by the window, the cold coming in off the glass. Eliza was grateful she had on a warm sweater and her woolens beneath it.

"Alright, what sounds good?" Phillip said, studying the menu.

"What do they have?" Eliza asked. A menu laced with Cyrillic letters stared back at her.

"I'd say everything from pork belly to sauerkraut, from the smell of it," Esme snarked.

"At this point ... don't care." Eliza closed the menu.

"Do you trust me?" Phillip asked, leaning in, his elbows on the red checkered table cloth.

Esme glanced at Eliza. "Do we?" Esme asked.

Eliza nodded. "Do your worst."

Phillip nodded and glanced up as the waitress returned, her notepad at the ready. "Let's see ... *ciorbă de burtă* for me ... *supă de pui cu tăitei* for Eliza. Chicken noodle soup is a safe bet. And for Esme, how about ... *fasole cu afumătură*. Sound good?"

"As long as you didn't order me pickled sheep brains, we're good," Esme was in a foul mood. *Hangry*. Eliza recognized the symptoms. Meanwhile, she felt drained, both physically and mentally.

Phillip and the waitress had a protracted exchange and while Eliza couldn't understand a word of it, she recognized the signs of a Casanova when she saw them. Sure, he'd been all sweet and understanding, quoting Shakespeare and offering kind advice 30 minutes ago at the hospital, now he overtly flirted with the staff.

"This oughta be good," he said, when the waitress headed back to the kitchen.

"What did you order for me?" Esme asked.

"You seem like a brave soul," he laughed.

"I'm not a picky eater," Esme concurred, "but I do have my limits."

"You're from the UK," he chuffed. "What do you think of haggis?"

"I don't have the guts for it," Esme winced. "Meanwhile, my sister could probably take down a whole haggis by herself."

Eliza shook her head. "It's a good day for soup."

"I thought it might feel good on your sore throat." Phillip turned to Esme and leaned in. "So tell us what you found in the hospital that seems to have Eliza so concerned?"

A quick look shot between the two women, but it wasn't of reserve. He knew of Esme's abilities and clearly wanted to know more. Eliza wondered if Esme was ready to talk about it yet. She'd tried to get her to open up before she'd stormed off to the car, but the emotions were still too raw.

"Well," Esme said, not sure where to begin. "In a way, my abilities are a bit like being a spiritual geiger counter, I suppose."

Eliza's brow arched. Leave it to her sister to put it in a way her engineer sister could understand. Esme continued, "I can sense there are spirits in that building, old souls trapped, held for ransom by history."

"Fascinating." Phillip rested his chin on his fist, his elbows still on the table. "Go on."

Esme complied and told him what she'd experienced at the hospital, pausing when the waitress came back with their drinks and again when their food arrived. The mood around the table changed visibly.

Eliza, who'd been sullen and dark most of the day, brightened at the sight of the large bowl of chicken noodle soup. The noodles were handmade, wide, thick, and long. Large chunks of vegetables and white meat floated in a golden broth. Steam rose from the bowl and perfumed the air around her. A large chunk of crusty bread and a plate full of butter pats came with it.

Esme peered into the ceramic crock that appeared to contain rich, savory beans with ribbons of smoked pork. She tasted it cautiously, but didn't hesitate to dive in once the stew hit her taste buds. Her hunger made manners unimportant as she practically shoveled the food to her mouth.

Phillip's countenance seemed hopeful until he dipped his spoon into the soup before him. The broth was cloudy, not quite brown, not quite clear. Off-white ribbons that were not noodles slithered off his soup spoon and slipped back into the bowl with a plop. He wrinkled up his nose and even Eliza recoiled as the distinct perfume of vinegar rose from the soup.

"What the hell is that?" Esme's face twisted with the same disgust painted on Phillip's face.

"You ordered the tripe soup." Eliza blanched at what floated in his bowl.

Phillip filled his spoon with broth and lifted it to his lips, taking a tentative sip, but didn't seem to enjoy it. "I ordered bravely," he said. "That's what matters."

"Bravery is noble," Eliza quoted, watching as he took another spoonful. He shoved it into his mouth and chewed, but again, his face gave him away.

"It also appears misguided," Esme smirked. "And slightly ... *chewy*."

"So, how is it?" Eliza couldn't resist asking.

Phillip had to force the bite down. A bead of sweat formed on his brow and upper lip. "It tastes like vinegar ... and regret."

The grey sky now hung heavy over the town. Drizzle fell in the lower elevations, and the cold seemed to have settled heavily in the valley where the town gazed up into the clouds and snow-circled mountain peaks.

Since they were too late to make it to the market before it closed, the waitress helped them out by packing up a supply of bread, pastries, and several offerings of more palletable soups for later meals. It helped the restauranteur, who didn't have to worry about wasting the leftovers, and ensured there would at least be something palatable to eat for the next couple of days.

They arrived at the farmhouse well after dark, and found Alban still sitting in the chair where he'd been ordered to remain. He stood, like any good soldier, when his commanding officer came into the room.

"Good man," Phillip observed. "At ease."

Clack, clack, clack.

Esme stood in the doorway, hesitant to enter the same room, knowing she might channel something she wasn't up to dealing with. She'd already had a stressful enough day, with so many lost souls pulling at her and demanding to be heard, their messages garbled and hard to translate. It was almost the same when she communicated with Alban, only not as intense.

"I think I'll turn in," she said to Eliza.

Eliza, busily cleaning out the refrigerator, paused. "I'll be up in a while," she responded. "I'm tired, but I know I won't sleep any time soon."

"If at all." Esme came over and put her arms around her older sister. "You worry me."

"Perhaps a warm bath and a cup of tea will be enough to settle me," Eliza responded.

"I wouldn't bet money on it." Esme tugged on her sister's braid. "See you tomorrow."

"What are you going to do with him?" Eliza asked when Phillip came in with a laptop and Alban following him.

"Sentry duty, I think," Phillip said, "He can guard the door."

Eliza shrugged. "Seems like mindless work."

"Then he's just the man for the job," Phillip chortled, setting up the computer, plugging it into the wall behind the table where it would be less of a trip hazard. The jab made Eliza bristle. He might be dead, but he wasn't stupid.

Phillip didn't seem to notice as he took a seat and Alban moved to stand at his elbow. Eliza took a step back, inspecting her Great Uncle.

He might have been a handsome fellow at one time. His hair, while dried and disheveled, had a hint of copper in the fluorescent light. His desiccated corpse smelled of the centuries and mouldering earth, but not worse than the tripe soup Phillip had forced down. The tip of his nose had turned black and rotted off, leaving a bit of a crater that made him look a bit like *He Who Shall Not Be Named* from Harry Potter. Though his eyes were hollow, there was no malice behind them. If anything, they reflected a childlike innocence Eliza found endearing. Pity would do neither of them any good.

"Alban, can you go stand by the door?" Eliza asked. "We're trying to work."

Clack, clack, clack. He didn't move.

"You heard the *captain*," Phillip said. "Her orders are my orders. Do you understand?"

Clack, clack, clack. This time he turned and went to the door, putting his back to it as he stood at attention.

"At ease, soldier," Phillip said, turning his attention to the computer as it powered up.

Eliza finished the chores she'd made for herself and put the last of the meals away, then made herself a cup of tea. She came over and sat by Phillip, scooting where she could see the screen.

"The Romanian National Library in Bucharest," he said. "It's part of an international cooperative with libraries all over Europe. I thought perhaps we might find something about this Night Doctor."

"I'll go get my laptop, too. Maybe there's something in the archives of the newspapers ..." Eliza turned.

"Good idea!"

Eliza glanced at the clock at the bottom of her screen and stifled a yawn. *Three o'clock and all's well.* Except it wasn't. Phillip had fallen asleep at his station, slumped over the table. His upper torso lay over his outstretched arm. Drool stained the sleeve of his shirt, and his five o'clock shadow was doing overtime. Alban stood unwavering behind him, guarding the door.

Eliza's internal clock told her she should have gone to bed hours ago, but the urge for answers drove her past her breaking point. She'd been through the archives of all the reputable newspapers in Romania, as well as some from Germany, Hungary, and Ukraine. The records in the World War II museum lacked the critical details she'd been looking for and somehow, she found herself perusing the old headlines from the local tabloid, the title of which roughly translated to *The Weekly Shocker*.

Every issue dating all the way back into the early 50s had a hyperlink to take it to either a Romanian version, or one translated into English. Eliza had made it to the May 18, 1974 issue when something caught her eye.

The Zlatna Zombie!
Local Boy Vanishes: Secret Experiments in the Asylum?
ZLATNA, ROMANIA—Deep in the forests of the Apuseni Mountains, a chilling mystery has gripped this quiet mining town, and it's one no one dares to say out loud.

*Seventeen-year-old **Tudo Benea**, a local apprentice mechanic and son of a copper smelter, vanished without a trace last month. His mother said he left* *their home after supper on 6 April to meet friends near the old train tracks. He never came home.*

Two weeks later, a shepherd from the neighboring village of Valea Mică claimed to have seen the boy with milky eyes and blackened veins wandering near the **Zlatna Institute for Nervous and Undesirables**—*an infamous mental hospital, known by many names in this region, surrounded by razor wire and local superstition.*

Locals say they've heard screams at night from within the hospital's lower halls. Others whisper about a foreign doctor who arrived during the Second World War, and never left. Some call him The Night Doctor, a name they say was passed around like a curse in the years after the Nazis retreated.

Government officials have inspected the Asylum a number of times over the decades, after multiple reports of inhuman treatment and medical experimentation persisted since the late 1940s.

Authorities at the Institute declined to comment. A government spokesman dismissed the zombie claims as rural hysteria and capitalist propaganda, but offered no new leads in the disappearance of young Tudo.

Meanwhile, back in Zlatna, a mother waits. Elena Benea lights a candle every night at her window, praying for her son's safe return.

Want more forbidden files from behind the Iron Curtain?

Next week: **Cursed Church Bells of Bistriţa: The Monestary that Screams Back!**

Eliza's heart flipped in her chest and a rush of adrenaline washed through her. "Phillip," she said, reaching over to shake her sleeping coworker. "Phillip."

"Huh?" He sat up, abruptly, looking around, slack-eyed and sleepy. "What?"

"You're not going to believe what I found."

9

THE COST OF FIRE

C aspar crouched beneath the collapsed retaining wall on the northern edge of the grounds, his coat blending with the mould-darkened stone. The moon filtered dimly through the clouds, casting the hospital in monochrome ... a shadow of what it once was, much like himself.

He'd seen the girl—Esme, the other one had called her—drift into the ruined lobby like a moth to embers. A psychic, no doubt. But more than that, she had *connected*.

Caspar dreaded the idea that Alban had been captured, and the girl had confirmed it. But she hadn't just *seen* Alban. She had *communicated* with him. Not through speech, Caspar knew. While the flesh, sinew, and bone of the Awakened could mend itself thanks to the relic, things that were unnecessary for basic locomotion—organs, fluids, and *unnecessary* muscles like vocal cords—shriveled up or rotted away over time.

But she, this Esme, possessed other senses. Senses that allowed her to hear the silent voices of his sons.

Alban had *spoken* to her.

The rituals must have done more good than Caspar knew. The thought brought tears to his eyes and a sensation to his heart that had been absent so long, he'd forgotten what it felt like: *hope*.

Caspar's breath caught and his stomach flipped at the thought. *She had heard Alban.* The others were voiceless since their Awakening. They followed commands, yes, but their souls had been locked behind a barrier he couldn't breach.

But Esme—she pierced it.

She could be the key.

He would take her, yes. She would understand, once he showed her the depth of his work, once he explained the nobility of his mission. He didn't want to hurt her. He needed her.

But first: escape.

Night fell hard and fast. Fog rolled in low, clinging to the forest floor and the skeleton of the sanatorium. It was the perfect night for what he had planned, and Caspar wondered whether God was finally answering the decades of prayers—or whether Pluto had finally been appeased. The theological dichotomy wasn't lost on the doctor, but he'd lost any real allegiance to faith the day the stray British bomb had destroyed his whole world.

Caspar returned to the fallout shelter through the circuitous rear passage, where tangled roots and rubble concealed his comings and goings. The Awakened stood waiting.

He touched each of their shoulders in turn, whispering their names like a benediction.

"Esteban, Francisco, Manuel, Tudo, Radu, Ansel, Antonio … come."

They moved slowly, since their awkward gait did not lend itself well to silence, winding their way through the maze of hallways that would take them out of the hospital at a location away from the dig site.

They almost made it.

The moment Caspar stepped into the clearing, he heard a commotion from the distant edge of the courtyard, echoed by a cry from another direction he couldn't pinpoint. The muffled thundering of running feet on earth and stone told him that the archaeological team had set a watch of not only their own site, but the entire hospital grounds. In his alarm, he dropped his valise, and papers spilled onto the earth. He gathered them quickly, shoving them back inside.

He cursed himself for not expecting it. Esme and the other one hadn't seemed like Covenant operatives, but perhaps they were. Or perhaps they were something else. At the moment, it didn't matter.

"*¡Agáchanse, se van a ver!*" *Get down or they'll see you!* It didn't matter that some of the Awakened didn't speak Spanish. They obeyed his intent, not his words.

The shouting in the dark indicated that the guards were converging on Caspar and his *family*. A flare turned the sky ghostly red as the three watchers ran at them from the west, brandishing axes and what looked like shotguns. They had armed themselves against zombies.

They didn't realize what they truly faced. It was too late for his sons to hide. "*¡Ataquen!*" *Attack!*

The Awakened surged forward without a sound. Esteban moved like a storm surge, bones cracking and mending mid-motion as he tackled the nearest Agent. Antonio crashed into another, his jaw dislocated from the impact but already snapping back into place as he crushed the guard's throat with one ruined hand.

Tudo hesitated—just a flicker of uncertainty in his glassy eyes—before he moved toward the last Agent, a short woman in a black coat who wielded an axe with the smoothness of one who had fought before.

Caspar watched in dismay as she sidestepped Tudo, bringing the axe down hard against his left leg. The wound would not kill him, but it would slow him until his muscles regenerated. He could not heal as fast as Esteban because the Blade's magic thrummed newer in his cells. He stumbled.

Then, the distant sound of voices raised in alarm. Others were coming.

"*¡Retírense! ¡Corran hacia el bosque!*" *Retreat! Run for the forest!*

The Awakened obeyed—every one of them but Tudo.

The boy had risen, but sluggishly. The wound was already closing. He looked toward Caspar as the woman advanced. Another Agent emerged from the brush.

Caspar's face twisted with anguish. The others would escape, but not his youngest son.

"*¡Tudo,*" he called, a father's pain in his voice, "*protocolo tres!*" *Protocol three!*

The boy's face twitched.

An instant passed. Then he nodded.

With jerky hands, he reached inside his pocket and pulled out a small, sealed glass vial containing a sliver of white phosphorus.

He bit the cap off.

Flame erupted, white-hot and searing, catching the fog and consuming Tudo in a blinding burst of light.

The surviving Agents staggered back, eyes wide with shock and horror.

Caspar did not look back. He disappeared into the trees with the rest of his sons, the light of the boy he had lost reflected in his eyes like guilt and fire.

Dr. Bogden Lázár turned his pickup truck into the driveway of the once-upon-a-time farmhouse now occupied by Dr. Thorpe and the Wren girls. He had called ahead and notified Phillip as a courtesy rather than showing up unannounced in the wee small hours. There'd already been enough excitement tonight. Turned out that the American was still awake anyway.

He turned off the engine and hesitated before getting out. He'd worked for the Order for nearly twenty years, but as an artifact consultant and archaeologist, not as a field Agent. If he wanted to advance and eventually be considered for Chief of Field Research, he'd have to know more about field operations than simple artifact retrieval. Despite the loss of one of the team tonight, he found a silver lining in the practical field experience he got this week. And with members of the Wren family present, no less! They had a direct line to the Grand Aegis's ear.

He tried to hide his ambition from his colleagues, but in his heart, he thrilled to think that years of hard work were leading somewhere other than a dusty crypt or mud pit. Maybe he could get an office with an ergonomic desk chair to compensate for what years of hunching over half-buried pottery sherds had done to his poor back. Dr. Lázár took a deep breath and wiped the smile from his face. It wouldn't do to be grinning like a fool while reporting the night's violence.

"I can order Alban into the far corner of the kitchen while Dr. Lázár tells us what happened," Phillip offered as Esme rubbed the sleep out of her eyes.

Esme shook her head, despite Eliza's stern look of concern. "No, Order Agents are his people, even more than we are. He should be informed about what happened, even if he doesn't fully understand. I can help him."

"It's too much for you," Eliza warned.

"I'll tell you what," Phillip suggested. "Why don't we put a time limit on it? Let's say ten minutes. Once Alban can process thoughts with Esme's help, I'll explain that it hurts her for him to speak through her for too long. Then Bogden can give his briefing, we'll get Alban's thoughts, and Esme comes back upstairs."

"Ten minutes might not be enough. Uncle Alban has been trapped for so long ..."

"Ten minutes might be too much." Eliza stepped closer to Esme, knowing that the youngest Wren wouldn't have the good sense to protect herself because her heart would overrule her brain every time.

"Ten minutes is what we have. No more, and maybe less if Esme is showing signs of distress." Phillip wasn't sure if he was mediating a family dispute or a tactical disagreement between team members. Reluctantly, though, both sisters nodded.

"Poor Claudio." Phillip shook his head sadly. "He was no security guard. He wasn't prepared to fight a chihuahua, much less an animated corpse. No offense, Alban."

"None taken, old chap," Alban responded through Esme. "The Awakened are strong. Not stronger than humans, really, but since there's no sense of pain to reel in one's actions ..." The pale grey shoulders shrugged.

"The Awakened?" Eliza asked.

"That's what he calls us. His Awakened sons. My memory is spotty, you understand. I only remember my active moments and not even all of those, if I'm honest. But I remember that. He sees the Awakened as his family."

"There were several of them, according to the surviving guards." Dr. Lázár couldn't believe his eyes. A corpse talking through a girl? Unbelievable. "Do you recall how many?"

"More than three. There was me, there was Esteban, and there were others. I wasn't able to think well enough to count or learn their names."

"But you know Esteban?" Eliza coughed once and sipped her tea to soothe her voice.

"At first there was only Esteban. Then, when I infiltrated the Covenant operation, I learnt that there had been others that the Nazis provided and forced the doctor to use. The Germans said they would burn Esteban if the doctor didn't comply. So he did. The Covenant liberated him, but then forced him to do the same."

"They threatened Esteban as well?" The tale enraptured Phillip.

"No, they offered Dr. E all the research they had on cults of Pluto. I'm not quite sure why, but it's related to the Blade. But then I was captured and Awakened, and I don't remember too many of the details after that. Just flashes, really."

Esme swayed in her seat, sweat beading on her furrowed brow.

"Enough," muttered Eliza under her breath. "Phillip, explain to him."

Dr. Thorpe nodded. "Alban, did you know that Eliza and Esme are your great-grandnieces?"

Alban sat on his chair, turning his filmy eyes to the exhausted girl. Had his face been intact, his expression might have been described as reverent.

"I don't know how long you can remember things once Esme goes away, but ..."

"I remember the silence, then the doctor. Caspar. Then the years when I wasn't ... anyone. Those are hazy."

Phillip crossed his arms, his jaw tight. "The link is impressive," he said, "but it's dangerous for her."

Alban's head tilted as he looked at his descendant. Esme's body shuddered once, involuntarily, and her head dipped.

"I don't mean to hurt her."

"I believe you," Phillip replied gently. "But you're not drawing power from her; you're drawing structure. She's holding your soul together like scaffolding. But it's too much for one person."

Alban remained quiet for a long moment.

"She's my blood." His borrowed voice trembled faintly with something between wonder and grief. "She walks through this world like it means something. As though it's not all broken. I remember that ... I remember *being* that."

Esme exhaled sharply, swaying where she sat. Eliza stepped forward.

"That's enough."

Alban turned and held her gaze. "If she is the light that lets me speak, then I will be silent for her sake until she summons me again, even if that day never comes."

He stood from his chair and gazed again at Esme. Then he squared his shoulders and walked toward the kitchen. When he reached the farthest corner, he turned to Phillip and the spark of recognition drained away, replaced by the spine-stiffened posture of the vigilant soldier awaiting orders.

Phillip stared at him for a long moment, feeling the tragedy of Alban's existence.

Esme fell back against the sofa cushions, barely conscious, the link severed like a flame snuffed.

Dr. Lázár had watched the entire exchange with his mouth agape. "Unbelievable."

10

THE LIES WE LIVE WITH

"There's more," Eliza said, placing a cup of tea in front of her sister, adding a pastry on a paper napkin. At this point, no one was going to bed any time soon. "I found something in a local tabloid."

"Are you kidding?" Esme said. "A tabloid?"

"I know." Eliza shrugged, turning her laptop toward her sister, hitting the button to awaken it. The article appeared on the screen. "Read."

Esme complied and squinted as she leaned in to study the document. "The Zlatna Zombie?" Her tone held obvious disdain. She continued reading, scrolling until she reached the end. "They make this poor boy sound like a monster. As if being undead wasn't enough of a curse. Did this writer even fact check a single thing?"

Eliza shrugged.

"They made him a headline. A ghost story. Not a missing boy. And if the Agents heard correctly last night, the poor child was undead for decades and then set himself ablaze on this Night Doctor's orders." She pushed the computer away, like she could feel the shame the author might not have experienced. Eliza shivered as she sensed her sister's empathy for the missing boy.

"Correct," Eliza stated, closing the laptop. "Clearly reticent to fact check."

"You might say the reporter was proudly intransigent in his ignorance," Phillip added, returning to the kitchen. "Due diligence is never a suggestion, but a mandate."

"I'll do it," Eliza said.

"Do what?"

"Ask the unasked."

"How?" Phillip asked, perhaps a bit too bluntly.

Eliza shot him a look to match her offense at the brutally obvious challenge. "I *can* speak."

"Not well." Phillip must have recognized her displeasure. "It just seems like it's such a strain on your voice to carry on even a simple conversation. Dr. Lázár wants us to come to the site of the attack last night. He got a call from one of his men that they found some documents you might find of interest."

"What documents?"

"They would appear to be pages from this Night Doctor's journal."

"Eliza's right," Esme said. "She needs to follow up on this article."

"Divide and conquer?" Eliza suggested.

"You can drop us off at the site and take the car." Phillip took the car keys from his pocket and laid them on the table.

"*Now* you're okay with it?" Eliza croaked.

"First off, I can see there's no arguing with the two of you," Phillip said. "Secondly, I hate lazy pseudojournalism almost as much as I hate vinegar."

Eliza dropped Phillip and Esme off at the site of the night's events, even before the sun broke over the tree tops. The drive to town gave her the first moment she'd had alone in several days, and it recharged her social battery to have silence fill the car. It was a beautiful, albeit chilly morning, and the fir trees seemed especially green after the recent rain. The brilliant colors of fall were painted in the blazing red maples and golden elms that trembled in the morning's light breeze.

In town, Eliza made her way to the city center where a proud gothic building stood with the official government seal over the door, the Romanian flag flying above the main entrance. Across the street a cathedral spire, clad in silver, probably aluminum, reached for the heavens. The clock at the top of the white brick tower heralded the hour as 8:00 am. Pulling into the car park and taking out her phone, she oriented herself to the locations noted in both English and Romanian.

She'd passed the bistro where they'd eaten the night before as she entered the town. The *Primăria Zlatna*, or City Hall, sat in front of her. The main office for *The Weekly Shocker* was just a few doors down. She pulled up the translation app Randall had recommended as part of her kit and typed in a few opening questions that might help her find the right person to speak with. If no one spoke English, she could use the translator to ask the questions, and record the answers for later transcription.

She donned her stocking cap and pulled it down over her ears as she stepped out into the sunshine and the biting wind. It seemed even colder here than at the farmhouse. She hurried down the street. Three doors down, she paused outside a glass door with gold lettering that looked like it had seen better days. In Romanian, it said, *Șocul Săptămânii. Redactor-șef: Mihai Corbea.*

She scanned it with her phone. The computerized voice translated it. *The Shock of the Week. Chief Editor: Mihai Corbea.*

This was the place. She pulled the door open and a bell rang over her head. She stepped into the 1950s-era office, replete with harvest gold and pumpkin orange decor, avocado green carpet and the heavy perfume of stale cigarette smoke and burnt coffee. A rotary fan spun lazily. A smoldering mug full of cigarette butts set next to the black rotary phone and an old fashioned *Rolodex*.

She stood there a moment, warming quickly. She pulled off her gloves and tucked them in her pocket.

A man came around the corner with his nose in a magazine, not seeing her. Then he looked up, stopping stone cold as if he hadn't heard the bell. Eliza studied him for a moment. He was rotund, with a thick head of hair and a mustache so bushy he looked like a walrus. The hair and mustache were both dyed an obscenely obvious black. The wrinkles around his eyes and sagging lids suggested a man much older than he wanted to admit.

„*Pot să vă ajut?*" he grunted. The translator picked up on it.

Eliza pulled up her first question. "Hello. I am looking for one of your writers, Radu Dorneau. Does he still work here?" The voice in her phone said it in Romanian.

The man narrowed his eyes at her. "Why are you looking for Radu? Does he owe you money?" The phone translated for her.

"No," Eliza typed in the follow up question. "I'm here about an article from an issue published in 1974 about the *Zombie of Zlatna*. I have some questions."

"Ah, The *Zlatna Zombie* ... What a classic! That piece got us blacklisted in three countries and a warning from the mayor's office." The man's moustache flinched. "Wait, are you police?"

"No," Eliza's thumbs typed her question quickly. "I'm a scientist working with the archeological team at the old *Spitalul de Recuperare Zlatna*. Are you the editor?"

"Mihai," he replied, nodding as he took a seat at the desk, motioning to the only other vacant chair across from him. The other chairs around the room's perimeter were stacked with files. How they hadn't toppled over was nothing short of a mystery in itself.

"Eliza Wren," she spoke for herself, as an introduction, before she sat down. She typed on her phone. "I'm more interested in what you didn't print."

He narrowed his gaze, studying her. "American?"

"British," she corrected, typing her next question. "Can you tell me more about the boy in the article? Tudo Benea."

Mihai exhaled, stubbing out a cigarette in the coffee cup overflowing with butts. "It wasn't just one boy. I knew the second one, Raul. He was my neighbor's son. He helped me deliver magazines. The whole village helped search for them, for Raul and Tudo." His voice cracked and she could see humanity beneath his facade as he fought for control.

The conversation continued between the editor and Eliza via the translator on her cell phone. It was a clunky way to communicate, but Eliza appreciated the ability to speak without straining her voice and was glad she'd thought of it on the long drive.

"I wouldn't write about him," he said. "Not Raul. Too painful. But that's not what I do anyway. "

"What do you do, Mr. Corbea?"

"I found it easier to write about Tudo and to say that the asylum took him. Ghost stories sell better than the truth ever could," he hesitated. "I only print what people can swallow."

Eliza tapped at her screen. "So, give me the whole meal."

He glared at her sternly. "I hope you're hungry."

Behind the crumpled blazer and tar-stained fingertips sat a man who never met a conspiracy theory he couldn't exaggerate. Too cheap and too paranoid to hire actual journalists, Eliza learned that *every* article published over the past 60-some years had come from this man, all written under a slew of pseudonyms.

He explained that his father had started printing papers during WWII to publish propaganda against the Nazis and through his own writing had convinced his fellow Romanians to turn from Axis automatons to Allies in every sense of the word. When he inherited the printing presses, he had other ideas of how to make a living.

"Every article I write is based on facts collected throughout the region. People tell me these stories in bars, cafes, and on the street. Every citizen of Zlatna knows the number of the tip line thanks to my cousin, Vasi."

"How so?" Eliza asked.

"He does all the marketing and distribution, sells subscriptions, and encourages the community to report anything unusual to the tip line"

"How did he get the number out so *quickly*?" The emphasis was completely lost in translation, but it didn't really matter. Eliza admired this business model, and the efficiency, or more accurately, sloth of the editor. If he were indeed a regular skin-flint, marketing seemed like the last thing he might spend money on.

"He coordinated with the local businesses to advertise in my magazine," he said. "He used a portion of the proceeds to print up stickers advertising the tip line number." Mihai laughed. "He even convinced a priest to post it in the confessional by donating a ham for the Easter feast at the rectory."

He reached into the desk drawer and tossed a stack of the stickers over to her. Eliza picked one up, studying it, then realized she'd seen the same sticker on the window of the cafe where they'd eaten the night before. Not speaking Romanian, she hadn't given it a second thought, not understanding the message it conveyed.

Interesting. But she had yet to ask the questions she really wanted to ask. "So, can I ask you about the young man that went missing? Tudo."

He nodded and sat back in his chair, the buttons on his faded striped cotton shirt strained against his stomach, dark hair appeared in the gaps. Eliza averted her gaze to her phone, typing in her questions, starting the next one before the translator finished conveying the first. "Where did you first hear about this boy going missing?" she asked. "Who told you about it?"

"I read an article in the newspaper," he said. "The police were looking for anyone who knew what had happened to the boy. I knew his mother, so I called her."

"You actually spoke to his mother?"

"She told me Tudo and his friend, Raul had gone camping but neither returned home when expected. That's when she called the police and reported him missing." He stood and went over to one of the chairs in the corner, filled with files. He rifled through the stack, talking with his back to her as he searched for something. "A few months later, they found Tudo's car found beneath a bridge near Moldova Valley. It'd gone off the road and over a ravine. A body was found burned beyond recognition. No one could tell if it was Tudo or Raul." He reached for a pack of cigarettes and started to light one up before he hesitated. Eliza knew he'd noticed her expression change, though she tried to control her face. She struggled not to break down coughing in the stale room, more smoke would only exacerbate her already fragile throat.

He put the pack away and reached for the coffee cup on the side table, pouring a thick black sludge from the carafe on the old Mr. Coffee, or whatever the Romanian equivalent was.

"So how did this go from a missing person's report to a tabloid story about zombies?" Eliza asked through her phone.

A wry smile appeared faintly beneath the mustache, his brow lifting ever so slightly. He took a drink of his coffee, coughed, then set the cup aside. "Well," he cleared his throat. "People talk."

Eliza furrowed her brow, shaking her head to encourage him to keep going. He did.

"This is a land of lore and legend. Vampires, werewolves, Nazis. That old nervous hospital was the place of nightmares when I was a boy. The Third Reich invaded the region and while my Jewish friends were being slaughtered and carted away, we hid in the tunnels trying to get a glimpse at what they were up to. And you know what they say, rumors only grow."

"Rumors you started?" Eliza typed.

"The truth doesn't sell, Miss Wren. But the lies we live with? Hell, those pay my rent," he said. "I have lived here my entire life and I've seen *things* ... things I can't explain. As an adult, I've tried to make sense of it. This is how I've been able to process the trauma of life in an occupied country. Besides, people know what they're getting when they buy my magazine. No one considers it gospel."

Eliza sat back for a moment, quietly absorbing what he might possibly mean, formulating her response. She took up her phone again. "Tell me," Eliza typed in. "What have you seen?"

11

THE SOUND BENEATH THE STONE

"We find these papers near the north side of grounds." Marta Horvath, a Hungarian-born member of the Order's archaeological team, handed a manila folder to Phillip. "Original is in Spanish, but we change for you."

"Ah, thank you, Marta. Your English is really improving. You weren't burned by the phosphorus, I hope?"

"No, thank you for ask, Dr. Thorpe. I am fine."

"Good, good." His eyes perused the age-yellowed notebook pages. It would have been fine if they'd left them in Spanish, honestly. He was a linguist, after all, and spoke Spanish, French, German, and Greek fluently, picking up Romanian here and there over the last few months. But the translation seemed adequate, so he didn't mention it. Marta nodded and returned to the dig site, leaving Phillip and Esme at a picnic table near the car park.

"What does it say?" Esme craned her neck to try and get a look at the documents.

"This first one is fascinating, from a scientific point of view. It looks like the Night Doctor is conducting some sort of kluged rituals to the Roman god Pluto, but he's treating them like experiments ... keeping records of how much of each herb he'd burned as offering, making observations, very detailed stuff." He extended the translated page to Esme carefully. "Are you sure you should touch this?"

"I'm empathic and clairvoyant, Dr. Thorpe, not psychometric." She took a moment to enjoy his confused expression. Certainly he knew what the words meant, but maybe not what their implication might be as far as she was concerned. "Yes, it's safe for me to touch them. It's possible I'll have a vision, but there's no way to know if an object will trigger it or not. The voices come when they come."

Phillip nodded uncertainly and relinquished the papers.

"Rosemary and basil? Was he making incense or dinner?" Esme puckered her lips in concentration.

"Rosemary was sacred to the Romans, often associated with immortality. The basil is a little more unusual, but I suspect it had to do with our Dr. Caspar trying to purify his conscience. Keep reading. There are two pages. One is clinical—cold, detached. The other is ... not."

Esme studied the ritual log first.

SUBJECT BACKGROUND:

IDENTIFIER: ANTONIO. MALE, APPROX. 34 YEARS AT TIME OF DEATH

CAUSE OF DEATH: HEMORRHAGIC TRAUMA TO CHEST CAVITY (UNVERIFIED ORIGIN)

STATE: AWAKENED VIA ARTIFACT APPLICATION (PROTOCOL I), 46 YEARS POST-APPLICATION

COGNITIVE FUNCTION: MINIMAL. OBEYS COMMANDS. NO SPONTANEOUS COMMUNICATION OR RECOGNITION.

CONTROL OBJECT: GOLD RING EMBEDDED IN STERNUM.

PLUTONIC RITUAL PARAMETERS:

INVOCATION: HYBRID CONSTRUCT OF ROMAN SUPPLICATION, DELIVERED IN LATIN. BLOOD-SALTING CIRCLE WITH SACRIFICIAL ASH.

CATALYSTS: GOAT'S BLOOD, FRAGMENTS OF OLIVE BRANCH BURNED IN TEMPLE-GRADE OIL, GROUND ROSEMARY AND BASIL, ONE BRONZE COIN (REPLICA, MARKED WITH PLUTO'S BUST.)

DURATION: 41 MINUTES. CONTINUOUS CHANTING, SIGIL TRACING, APPLICATION OF ARTIFACT TO FRONTAL CORTEX AT PRE-DESIGNATED INTERVALS. (3X)

OBSERVED REACTIONS:

3:53 - SUBJECT'S LEFT HAND SPASMS. NO EXTERNAL STIMULUS APPLIED.

3:56 - AUDIBLE GRUNT. LOW FREQUENCY, ORIGIN UNDETERMINED.

3:58 - RIGHT EYE TWITCHES. OPENS BRIEFLY. SCLERA VISIBLE. NO PUPIL DILATION.

4:08 - ARTIFACT BLADE PRESSED TO MEDIAN BROW. NO VISIBLE DERMAL REACTION. THE SUBJECT'S MOUTH OPENS. NO LANGUAGE DISCERNED.

4:14 - SUBJECT CEASES MOVEMENT. RE-ENTERS PASSIVE STATE.

CONCLUSIONS:

THE SUBJECT DISPLAYED GREATER REACTIVITY THAN BASELINE DURING RITUAL. WHETHER THIS IS DUE TO INVOCATION CONTENT, ARTIFACT RESONANCE, OR OTHER FACTORS IS UNCERTAIN.

ATTEMPTS TO COMMUNICATE FAILED. THE SUBJECT IS UNWILLING OR UNABLE TO SPEAK. UNCLEAR IF SUPPRESSION IS DUE TO PHYSICAL DECAY, POSTMORTEM COGNITIVE FRAGMENTATION, OR METAPHYSICAL INTERFERENCE.

Esme flipped to the original version of the document. "He was trying to talk to them. But he can't. And he doesn't know why."

Phillip shook his head. "They can follow commands, and that's it. They aren't like Alban."

"But they're like he was. Before you pulled the tags out of him. Look." She pointed at the words *control object*. "Without the control object, he can't control them. But he can't reach them either."

"The Blade left them between life and death," he commented, "and Caspar's been trying to make their way back ever since. Look here." He indicated the other page, a few scribbled lines in a far less precise hand.

"*They told me they were prisoners. But I still opened them. Still cut. Still watched. How many cried out before the Blade changed them? Before those in power burned them? Am I their shepherd? Their warden? Their murderer?*"

"He hated what he did, but he still did it. Maybe he's still doing it now." Bile burned the back of her throat as she thought of the Blade's victims—Caspar's victims.

Phillip took the papers back from her. "Can we try an experiment of our own? You were able to sense them yesterday. Can we step back inside the lobby and see if it feels different to you now?"

Esme nodded, still aching with the thought of all who had suffered. She rose, following Phillip back to the archway that led to the hospital's reception area. He hesitated at the door, motioning for her to go first.

She stepped through the old entrance, her boots crunching on the detritus of decay. She paused at the center of the ruined lobby. Her breath caught.

She filtered out the memory-echoes this time, her mind breezing past the sadness of the nurses and the frightened pulses of long-forgotten patients. Underneath all that lay something else. Something deeper.

A hum, like a vibration under her skin. A low, pulsing pressure in her bones.

She frowned. "Something's still here. But it feels different than yesterday. Quieter, but more ... aware. Like Alban, but not like him, too. He speaks in my head, but this ... this is just waiting." Despite her heightened senses, neither of them noticed the observer watching them from the shadows of the damaged hallway.

"Were any of the Awakened left behind?"

"It's hard to say. I don't think he would leave them. But there's less static now. They taste like static."

Suddenly, ACDC's "Thunderstruck" cut the dusty air. Startled, Phillip extracted his cell phone from his trouser pocket. "Oh, it's Eliza. If she's calling instead of texting, she must have found something important." He tapped the green *answer* button. "Hello?"

"Hey, I ... paper ... kid ... guy said ..." Eliza rasped, her voice punctuated by blips of silence.

"Hold on a sec, Eliza. Let me step out of the concrete box. Are you okay here for a minute, Esme?"

The younger sister nodded, listening to the silence around her.

"I'll be right back. I'll be just over here. Holler if you need anything." Phillip stepped back out of the archway and down the steps so he could get better reception. It was hard enough for Eliza to say something once, much less repeat herself.

Esme nodded again, barely hearing him. The hum had grown louder. It wasn't in the walls; it was *behind* them. She turned her gaze to a side corridor, long abandoned and half-collapsed. She took a step, and then another.

The light faded quickly here. Dust floated in the air and the plaster flaked off the bones of the structure. The hum called to her. Not words exactly, but acknowledgement and *intent*. She could feel it pulling at her thoughts, like a dream she couldn't quite remember.

The Blade. It had to be the Blade.

Maybe it had been dropped like the papers, left behind in the rush to escape. Maybe she could recover it and at least Caspar couldn't use it anymore. Maybe ...

She didn't see the movement in the shadowed alcove until it was too late.

A hand clamped over her mouth and another one snaked around her torso. She struggled, kicked back, even as the acrid chemical sting filled her mouth and nose and the world began to blur.

"Shh, child. You're going to help us all." The voice, gentle and low, cracked with time.

Caspar.

She saw his face—lined with sorrow, but wild with certainty. Then everything went dark.

The last thing she felt was her knees buckling and something lifting her like she was a sleeping child. The world faded to black, and the Blade's hum surged through her like a heartbeat she could no longer control.

Outside, Phillip cursed under his breath. "Eliza, say that again? No wait, just text me. The signal here is complete crap. We'll meet you back at the farmhouse."

He turned, looking back toward the hospital entrance, immediately registering that something amiss.

"Esme?"

No answer.

12

A BIRD WITHOUT WINGS

Eliza had stopped at the market for a few essentials. A proper tin of tea—loose leaf, oolong— nestled against the cream and a few other staples as she walked from the market back to Phillip's car. They would be small comforts for the chill of an autumn night. She'd even picked up a different brand of coffee, hoping Phillip might be willing to switch to something less ... *skunky.*

As she walked, she paid more attention to her surroundings beyond the architecture, noticing the stickers from the tabloid stuck to light poles and in windows. Most showed signs of age, fading and cracking. She spotted a bulletin board on one of the closed-up cafes where an old menu had been covered with photographs and flyers of missing persons.

She paused to study them. Many of them were decades old. Photographs included an aging polaroid with writing on the white frame at the bottom. *Persoană dispărută. Sunați dacă ați fost văzută.*

Eliza reached for her phone and scanned the picture with her translator app. *Missing Person. Call if seen.* A phone number Eliza now recognized as that of the tabloid's tip-line was included on the photograph.

From her interaction with Mihai Corbea, she knew he was essentially the pivot point for information in the region. Everyone knew to call him with anything unusual, but also, he served as a contact point for his neighbors. No one had to give out their number because Mihai would be able to put them in touch with the authorities if a legitimate clue came in.

This served double duty. It prevented the families from getting their hopes up. It saved them the heartbreak of thinking their loved one might come home, especially when the likelihood seemed grim. Self-serving on his part, maybe, because he always got the first scoop on a story. It also allowed him to serve his community, and to give back.

There were so many missing. So many families hoping against all hope.

Thoma Verge, 17, last seen May 9, 1967

Jaromir Mirislav, 22, last seen February 14, 1969

Francisco Feraru, 34, last seen January 25, 1971

Vladimir Patchenko, 19, last seen June 5, 1996

Tudo Benea and Raul Cernat.

The grainy color copy of a picture on the faded flyer made her pause. They were just boys, younger than Esme, and just as innocent.

Tudo wore a mustard and brown tank top with shorts that were cut too short, but indicative of the mid-1970s. Raul wore a white tee with a red band around the collar and sleeves. Red swim trunks finished the ensemble.

They were pictured leaning on a yellow panelled station wagon, their arms around each other's shoulders. Tudo gave a thumbs up sign with his other hand. Raul flashed two fingers to symbolize peace. Eliza's heart tightened in her chest, as her gaze scanned some of the other names and photographs.

Ansel Hossu

Antonio Groza

Luca Rădu

It struck Eliza that they were all young men, roughly the same age, height and build as Alban. *What was the connection? Was there a connection? Or was it random?*

Eliza took out her phone and snapped a few pictures of the board, zooming in on each of the missing persons posters, flyers and photographs. They might be useful.

She glanced at her watch and realized the daylight would be fading soon. She had as many questions as she did answers, but they would have to wait for another time. She needed to get back and see what Esme and Phillip had found.

She and Phillip had exchanged a few messages since their brief phone conversation earlier, and the last one had her on edge. It'd simply said, *Forget the farmhouse. Come to the hospital site.* Something about that seemed unusual. She'd tried calling him for clarification, but it went straight to voice mail.

All through the long drive back, her mind buzzed with information and she fretted about what had Phillip sending such cryptic messages. Then, there was the story of the missing boy. The bizarre occurrences surrounding the *nervous hospital*, as Mihai so charmingly called it. Threads of rumor, history, and unease tangled in her thoughts as she drove. The late-afternoon sun burned through the thinning canopy overhead, gold and relentless. It warmed her body and soul.

Excitement quickened her pace, driven by her eagerness to share what she'd learned with Esme and Phillip. Restlessness propelled her forward knowing she'd discovered something real. Something of use.

But the minute she turned into the site's gravel drive, her pulse shifted. She knew *something* was ... *really wrong*. She got out of the car, and she heard her sister's name being called in the wind, first from the north, and then from the east. *Essmmmeeee*! The voices echoed in the trees, like a child searching for a lost dog.

Eliza scanned the clearing, looking for her sister, expecting to see her come bounding out of the tunnel at the sound of her name. Even though Esme had a dark shadow in her soul, most of the time she was a bluebird of happiness, especially when they were doing anything together.

However, it was Phillip who appeared from the hospital's main entrance. He looked distraught. Eliza immediately put the pieces of the puzzle together. The wind shifted. The air stank of smoke and fear, and something worse ... *silence* where Esme should have been.

Their eyes met, and they both froze for a moment. Fearing the worst, anger flashed in her heart, flamed in her cheeks. Her heart flipped and leapt into her throat.

Eliza stormed across the clearing, boots crushing over broken glass and gravel. "Where ... is she?" Eliza's voice cracked with her fury.

Phillip turned, his face pale, his team scattered like debris in his wake. He caught Eliza by her arms, steadying her, lowering his head, his dark eyes drilling into her soul. "I went outside to talk to you when you called earlier today, but when I went back inside, she was gone."

"You *lost* my sister?" The words burned in her throat like a blade, digging deeper into her displaced heart. To be without her sister felt like being a bird without wings. They were a team. She *needed* Esme. Being apart was unbearable for both of them.

When Eliza left to go to college, Esme had been beside herself. Eliza hadn't been much better. The two talked on the phone every day until one Friday afternoon, Esme didn't answer her phone. Eliza called their mother, frantic.

"Esme didn't come home from her art class this afternoon," her mother informed her. *"Father's gone to drive the path. I'm calling her friends to see if maybe she went to someone's house and forgot to tell us."*

"Esme doesn't have any friends," Eliza remembered her own words vividly. *"I'm her friend. She doesn't need anyone else."*

"Of course your sister has friends," her mother snapped. *"We'll find her, Eliza. Don't worry about anything. She had plans for this weekend and she wouldn't miss them."* That worried Eliza most. Being habitually on time was a Wren family trait.

Esme turned up at Eliza's dorm room a little over an hour later. She'd taken some money from the cedar chest where she collected all the proceeds from her paintings father sold to his friends, and used it to take a bus to Paddington Station, then buy a train ticket.

It had been the worst hour of Eliza's life, but the best weekend they'd had, just the two of them. Once Esme got out of the dog house with their parents, weekends together at Oxford became a regular event for the sisters. Eliza would take the train to Paddington Station and meet her, so she didn't have to travel alone. Their parents funded the extra expense and considered it a savings from heartbreak and worry.

Eliza scowled at Phillip. "I told *you* ... keep her safe." Her voice broke and she felt her knees trembling.

"She probably just wandered off," Phillip said. "There's a breach from the north side, a mine shaft we didn't even know existed. Eliza, I swear, we'll find her."

Eliza's face twisted in fury. "Save it." Her voice cracked. "I trusted you. That's ... on me."

She stormed out of the entrance of the tunnels, fury burning in her soul, hands ripping at her hair, yanking her braid into twisted chaos. Phillip barked orders to his crew behind her, the echo reverberating from the tunnel.

The excitement of her day and of finding clues to the mystery at hand had been replaced with a conflagration of emotions she couldn't name. Esme did have a habit of wandering off sometimes when the visions carried her away, but she always returned, and Eliza could sense when to be worried. She was worried now. This wasn't normal for her sister.

*How could she have trusted **him**?* He clearly wasn't up to the job! It was a simple thing she asked, and something any first-year rookie should have been able to manage!

A pained cry escaped from her throat and her knees buckled. She found herself face first in a pile of damp leaves, weeping with fear and grief. Esme was too fragile to endure something like this alone. Eliza sobbed her sister's name, a weak cry.

"Eliza!" Phillip called, finally coming after her.

Warm hands collected her and lifted her from the litter of the forest floor. "Come on," Phillip steadied her, his voice soft. "You're no good to her like this. I've got every member of the archeological team looking for her. We're good at finding lost things. We'll find your sister."

He led her over to the picnic table where he'd sat with Esme earlier in the day. He took a handkerchief out of his jacket pocket and pressed it into her hand, encouraging her to dry her eyes. "Pull yourself together, and we'll go take over the lead. We'll find her, Eliza. I promise."

"You promised to protect ..." Eliza sniffed, drying her eyes on his handkerchief, studying the blue embroidered initial in the corner. "You said ..."

"I know," he pulled her into him, her head pressed to his chest. "And I'm sorry."

She let him hold her a moment, but it only served to fan the flames. Eliza pulled away and flung herself to her feet, rounding on him, fury burning with the tears in her eyes. "I ... don't ... want ... *sorry!*" she choked out the words. "I want ... my sister!"

Phillip bit his lip and nodded, standing. "Then let's go find her."

High above, in the skeletal bones of a crumbling watchtower, a figure stood cloaked in shadows, unmoving as he gazed out over the trees into the yard where a picnic table sat in the brown grass. Through binoculars he'd found among the mortal's things a decade ago, he'd been watching most of the day, his attention drawn by the commotion of the excited workers calling out a name he didn't recognize. *Esme.*

Now, a second woman came to the site, clearly upset. The man who'd been leading the team at the archeological site by the hospital called her by name. *Eliza.*

He began to put the pieces together. As a *Watcher*, he had a duty to monitor and to report. He had done so for centuries, remaining hidden in the shadows, spoken of in whispers. This region had been his home for centuries. He guarded it now even as he always had.

The ageless contest between the Order and the Covenant had been ramping up in recent years, as had tensions between the immortal factions. The avatar of the Covenant had fallen and their Champion had left the fold. Now the Order's own players were gaining strength.

He had heard the prophecy from the Father of Knowledge, of the woman with fire in her veins, and her sister pulled into the darkness. They had potential to become a dangerous pair. *Two turtle doves.*

He smiled, just barely.

"So, they've entered the game," he chortled to himself. "The *Father* will be quite interested to learn of this new development."

13

DEAD WEIGHT

C old stone pressed against her cheek.

Esme stirred, vision shifting in a blur of shadows and dust. She shivered in the darkness. The air was thick with the metallic scent of rust and something else—something that made her stomach clench even before her memory returned.

Caspar.

The chloroform.

She sat up too fast, and nearly toppled over. She wasn't bound, but her limbs felt heavy, the way they did when she awoke from a particularly vivid vision. Her head hurt like that, too, but fuzzier, thicker than after a vision. All of her senses felt as though they were wrapped in cotton.

She tried to examine the chamber, but it was too dark to see anything but the dimly-lit entryway. The weak light told her that a battery-powered lantern lay just outside the room where she found herself.

She listened to the world around her. The suffocating silence broken only by the occasional groans of wood settling and the distant dripping of water told her that she was underground, possibly in an unfinished cellar.

Using the moist stone walls to support herself, she struggled to a standing position as quietly as possible. She crept with painstaking slowness toward the light.

Three steps more. Two ... and then she felt it. A whisper of a sensation, like static on a dead channel pulsed behind her eyes. Faint. Familiar.

The Blade.

And more than that ... the *others*.

The Awakened were near. Esme shivered.

One more step and she'd be able to see what lay beyond the doorway framed in rotting timber—but she wasn't sure she wanted to know. Her heart pounded against her ribs. *That's it. If I get out of this alive, I am DONE with tunnels*. First in Dover where they'd found the Veil and Esme had very nearly lost her sister ... and now this.

The thought of Eliza drove her forward. *How worried she must be!* She crouched down and poked her head through the archway where the blue-white glow of a camp lantern illuminated a few feet in each direction. It was a tunnel, alright, a tunnel with a very distinct slope to the ground. And if she'd learned anything in Dover, she'd learned that *up* meant *out*.

She reached down and grabbed the lantern's handle, then turned to survey the chamber in which she'd awakened. It resembled a man-made cave of about four square metres, with ceilings low enough that her brother Elias would have to tilt his head to make sure not to whack it on the support beams that provided questionable bracing.

Her eye gravitated to the metallic glint of a brass bowl set atop a rotting crate in the corner. The chamber was otherwise bare, so it must be there for a reason. Her curiosity won out over her better sense, and she stepped over and held the lantern over the vessel, which appeared to be filled with coarse white powder.

"It is chalk." The sudden sound of a voice behind her made her cry out in alarm, and she whipped around to find a man standing in the doorway. "You are safe, Miss Esme. All will become clear soon."

"You're ... you're the doctor." It wasn't a question.

He took a step toward her, and she shrunk back. "You need not fear me, Esme. I apologize for the rudeness with which you were brought here, but there was no other way, you see." He shrugged his narrow shoulders. Esme would have put him at maybe 55 years old, even though she knew him to be closer to 130. "I was a doctor once, but the Nazis and the Covenant took that from me. You know the story of Dr. Frankenstein? They made me more like him."

Despite her terror, Esme empathized with the sadness in the man's eyes. She remembered her vision: the guilt he felt, the responsibility and duty to the Awakened. She searched for the right thing to say to him, to keep him talking. "They gave the Blade to you?"

His salt-and-pepper eyebrows rose in surprise. "You know of the Blade? How are you aware of this? You must not be from the Covenant, or you would know the answer to this question. So who are you?"

The question felt like a trap. She knew she mustn't to reveal too much. "I am not Covenant, no."

He studied her with his dark eyes, taking her measure. He seemed to decide something. "You have learned this from Alban." He studied her, watching for a reaction.

"Yes," she answered simply.

"How do you do this? I know he cannot speak. He has no ..." The Night Doctor touched his neck, searching for the right word. "... voice cords."

"Vocal cords," she corrected before she could stop herself. "No, he doesn't."

"I know this." Frustration knitted his brow and betrayed the tension in his energy. "Please explain. I have not brought you here to harm you. I have brought you so you can help them—help us."

"You mean the Awakened. You think I can help them?" The prospect of helping Uncle Alban and the others, so brutally suspended between life and death, tugged at her.

He seized on her question. "I believe you are the key. You can talk to them. You can tell me if the rituals are helping them. He told you my name for them, yet he cannot speak. Please explain this." His desperation rolled off him in waves.

She wanted to help. Esme always wanted to help. But Eliza's voice reverberated in her head, telling her not to trust so much. Not to be foolish. "I can be his voice." It was a vague answer, and obfuscation, the only weapon she had. Lying seemed unwise.

"Please go on. How is this accomplished? I have not observed these complex thoughts in my sons."

"Your sons?"

"They are my responsibility. They have become my sons, though only one was born so."

Esme nodded. "I can help him think. Then I can speak for him. I'm not quite sure how it works."

Caspar began to pace, thinking, weighing her words. When he turned back to her, his face wore a wild smile. "You must talk for Esteban. You must help him think, too."

"I ... I'll try. But my head really hurts. Can I have some water? And it's so cold here ..." Maybe if she could stall a bit, Eliza would find her. No doubt she was already looking.

"Ay, I am sorry. I do not feel these things the way you do. I will get you a coat and some water. I will come back with Esteban. But you must give me the light. I do not hunger or thirst very much, but I still need light to see."

"You don't mean to leave me here in the dark?" Horror filled Esme's tone.

Caspar's jaw set. A grimness passed across his angular features and he began to pace again.

"I want to help you," she began, trying to negotiate carefully the way Eliza or Elias would, "but I can't do that if I'm an ice lolly or if my head's coming apart. I'm willing to try and talk to Esteban, but I need some help, too. You simply *cannot* leave me in complete darkness after knocking me out and making off with me, and then expect me to be a good sport about everything. I am not a Nazi. I am not Covenant. I am just a person. Please treat me as one." The conviction in her own voice surprised her.

He was surprised, too. In the cold LED light, she could see the man he had been struggling with the madness that had infected him. He stopped pacing and stared into the emptiness of the chamber, his lips moving silently. Esme knew what that meant.

"You hear whispers, too?" she asked without thinking.

His head snapped to look at her, his eyes narrowing for a moment. Then he took a deep breath and straightened his posture. "Only one, Miss Esme. Very well, follow me and we will get you a coat."

The tunnel narrowed as Esme followed Caspar. She realized that they were in an abandoned mine. Eliza would have an absolute fit if she knew Esme was being held somewhere so unsafe. The air grew colder, dense with mineral dust. Esme shivered, and the chattering of her teeth reminded her of Uncle Alban.

Oh, what he's been through, she thought. *Maybe I can learn something here that can help him.*

Caspar picked his way along, his uncertainty of movement betraying the fact that he had only come here recently. She wasn't sure if that would work against her or in her favor. He stopped near a rusted iron doorframe, part of a collapsed storage chamber now converted into his makeshift quarters. He handed Esme a heavy overcoat—only a little too large for her—and a bottle of clean water.

"I didn't want any of this," he said quietly, ashamed. "I was a healer. But they turned me into a tool ... like the Blade."

Esme said nothing, though she took the water gratefully. Her hands trembled as she sipped.

He leaned his forehead against the oxidized metal, his eyes closed. "The Nazis and the Covenant, they both used me. The Nazis found Esteban and me after the bombs dropped on our town. At first they promised to protect us, but it wasn't long before they threatened us if I did not satisfy their curiosity about the Blade. So many prisoners they brought me ..." He paused, the memory still fresh and painful.

"The Covenant had infiltrated their ranks, you see. Hitler was wild about finding occult artifacts, and they watched and waited. Not to help the Nazi cause, but to steal the artifacts and replace them with fakes. Clever, no? When they found out about me, about Esteban, they stole *us*. By then, Alban and Ansel and two other Jews whose names I did not know were among the Awakened. I insisted that the Covenant take them as well, and I gave them names: Francisco and Manuel. They promised me freedom and unlimited resources to conduct research to find out how to help my boys. To find the right ritual to appease Pluto. It is his magic on the Blade, you see. But when they began insisting on human experimentation—just like the Nazis had—I resisted. They said if I did not do as they wished, they would burn Esteban. So you understand ..." He raised his eyes to her. "... I had no choice."

His expression reflected genuine pain. "They kept sending me prisoners, dissidents, people who had displeased their High Seer. Anyone they deemed expendable. I thought if I succeeded—if I could understand the Blade—that I could end the cycle and free us all. I could bring them back. I could bring *him* back."

Esme's gaze drifted to the far corner of the chamber where Esteban stood still as a statue. His clothes were tattered, and in the dim light, she could see a tell-tale scar just below his ribs. A scar like Alban's. The control object must be within.

The Blade's hum throbbed in the back of her skull. It was stronger here—angry, even. She could feel its hunger. It craved the experiments, the rituals, the pain. It saw each victim as a sacrifice, an offering to its angry god. It had no morality—only purpose.

Caspar straightened and crossed the room to Esteban. "He is the first ... Awakened by a horrible series of accidents. Please, try to speak to him. See? He listens to you."

Esme hesitated, then nodded. She reached out with her mind the way she had with Alban. She slowed her breathing, focused her energy.

Nothing. Only static.

Esteban's face didn't change. He stared *through* her, not *at* her. He was an empty vessel.

She knew why, of course. The control object still within him created a wall between his reality and theirs. Alban became freed when his tags were removed. That object ... it wasn't just a connection—it was a lock. And Caspar ... he didn't know.

She opened her eyes and shook her head. "I'm sorry. I can't reach him."

Caspar's expression hardened, a flash of madness sparking behind his grief. "You *have* to."

"I can't," she repeated, her voice firmer. "I would if I could. I'm sorry."

The doctor turned sharply to Esteban. "*Restringirla*. Restrain her."

Before she could move, Esteban crossed the chamber and gripped her arms with cold, unyielding hands. He held her fast—not violently, but like a vice at his father's command.

Esme's breath caught. Her fear rose ... not only for herself, but for what Caspar might become.

Caspar trembled in frustration. "I brought you here because you were the key. You *heard* Alban. I know you can help. But if you will not—even if you cannot—then you are just another failure on my list."

She tried to speak, but the air thickened. The Blade's hum surged, deeper now. More intentional. It was speaking to her through the sensation of pressure.

And she understood. It wanted her.

And beneath that craving, there lurked something more primal. *Not you alone. The one who has crossed the veil. The one who died.*

Eliza.

The Blade had felt Eliza. It *knew* her. It knew what she was, that she had stood on the edge of Death's domain and returned. To the Blade, she was not only valuable, she was perfect.

The ultimate sacrifice to its dark master.

"You're being used again," Esme whispered.

"What did you say?"

Esme licked her lips, buying time. "You're trying to bring life back. But the Blade doesn't serve life. It serves Pluto. You're not its master, you're its servant."

Caspar stared at her silently.

Then slowly he turned away, muttering to himself. "No, no ... I'm close. So close. She just doesn't understand yet. She'll see. She has to."

Esme looked to Esteban, searching for any sign at all, but saw only emptiness. A hollow shell waiting for a command.

She swallowed hard. She had to find a way to remove the control object. Or Eliza would die. Again.

14

More Than Just Footprints

P hillip escorted Eliza—too weak with worry to be left alone—back to the car. The teams were exhausted from the day's search. The sun had long since set and the night grew cold. The perfumed promise of snow lay heavy on the mountains around them.

Hours ago, he'd made a call for aid, and search and rescue teams were on their way. It might be hours before the additional personnel came; it could easily be dawn before the search dogs arrived.

"We should go back to the farmhouse," Phillip said, getting in the driver's seat beside her. "Maybe she found her way there."

Eliza sat with her head down, wisps of hair escaped from her braid, her nose and eyes red from tears and cold. Fatigue drew deep lines in her cheeks beneath her eyes. "I won't ..." she started, her throat constricting and swallowing her voice. "Won't leave her."

"But if she's at the farmhouse?" Phillip started, but froze when she looked up at him, her tear-stained face and fury-filled eyes confirmed what he feared. She would not leave her sister.

As she turned away, she stopped suddenly, and reached down for something she'd left in the cupholder. It was a sticker, one Mihai had given her. She'd told Phillip about her conversation with the tabloid's editor, and about the stickers.

"What if ..." she started, but didn't have the strength to continue. Her tears fell renewed and he knew she'd put the pieces together. So many missing young men, and now, her sister, too. Just like the men.

"Esme doesn't fit the profile," Phillip reached over and took her hand. "It's easy to associate her being gone with what's been happening around here for what would seem like decades. We have no evidence to associate Esme's disappearance with these missing persons cases."

"Don't we?" Eliza managed. She took out her phone, the battery almost in the red, and typed out a message in English, translated it into the local dialect, then texted it to the number. A painfully long moment later, a message came back.

Voi fi acolo dimineața. Eliza copied and pasted it back into the translator. "I'll be there in the morning."

Eliza glanced at Phillip as the phone read the message, her brows knitted and a fresh tear rolled down her cheek. "Morning?"

Phillip took her hand. "Eliza, everyone needs rest. You need rest. You need to eat and get some sleep. We can't help Esme like this. You know that. Your sister is a trained Aegis Agent. She's strong and she's coming back to you. I know she is. You have to have faith in Esme. She'd want you to take care of yourself, wouldn't she?"

The conviction in Phillip's voice caused her to consider his words, and find the truth in them. He was right. Esme wouldn't want her to keep going if it meant Eliza's health would be put in jeopardy. It'd been just over a year since Maelis' blade cut Eliza's life short. But she came back from the void beyond the veil. She could only pray Esme was far from the void, that she'd found shelter and would make her way back.

With no other option, Eliza simply nodded and reached for her seatbelt.

Phillip heated up some of the food she'd brought back with her from the market earlier, but Eliza wasn't hungry and didn't eat much. As soon as the few dishes were washed and put away, she started for her room, but stopped when Alban stood from his chair and moved to block the walkway. Eliza went to sidestep him, but he moved to block her. His teeth clacked and Eliza glanced up at him, seeing the question in his foggy eyes. A deep concern blanketed his countenance, a sympathy that one didn't have to be psychic to recognize.

"Esme is missing," she said, as Phillip came up behind her.

"What's wrong?" he asked over her shoulder, addressing Alban more than Eliza.

"Alban seems to be able to recognize that something is wrong." Eliza moved to pass, but a hand caught her arm and it wasn't Phillip's. She glanced down at Alban's grasp, his fingers gripping her lightly, communicating the most human sense of compassion. Eliza matched his gaze and nodded her acknowledgement of the sentiment, and Alban's hand released and he allowed her to pass.

"Don't worry, old chap," Phillip said behind her. "We'll find her."

Clack, clack, clack.

A hot shower provided some relief, and having her pajamas on while her hair dried provided a measure of comfort—comfort that Esme didn't have. It was gut-wrenching to think about where she might be, and Eliza's mind went to every worst-case scenario she could think of. And she could think of many. There had to be some help they hadn't thought of. Someone she could call?

Randall! Of course! Why hadn't she thought of him? Tossing the towel off her head, she went and got her phone off the charger. Not even bothering to check the time, she dialed his number.

"Eliza?" His voice sounded groggy, her name heavy with sleep. "What's wrong? It's after midnight."

"Esme ... missing." She could barely get the words out. She could hear fumbling on the other line, and the affronted hiss Faraday made when he was abruptly displaced while napping. She could picture him curled up on Randall's pillow beside his head, as he often did when the cat slept with her.

"Tell me everything," he said. "Slowly. Don't strain your voice."

Eliza recounted everything that had happened over the past twenty-four hours, about meeting Alban and Esme communicating with him in a way only her sister could. The Archivist's fingers tapped on the keyboard. He must have gone into his office to jot down notes. They were supposed to keep detailed field notes, but Eliza hadn't sat down with her journal to document anything since before she went into town.

"Search and Rescue have been called?"

"Yes," Eliza said. "Here ... tomorrow."

"That's good," Randall said. "Where are you now?"

"Farmhouse."

"Is Phillip Thorpe with you?"

"Downstairs," she answered.

"I'll check in with him in the morning and provide some additional resources for the rescue teams. We'll find her, Eliza. Your only job right now is to stay calm, and be patient. There's a method to search and rescue that is based on behavioral science and psychology—two fields I am certain you are more than familiar with. The panic factor can only delay their efforts so I beg you not to panic. I know it's hard, but you're a logical woman and we need you to be clear-headed if you're going to be of any aid to your sister. Okay?"

"Yes," Eliza swallowed the word.

"This isn't a one-size-fits-all methodology," Randall continued. "A multitude of factors can influence how an individual reacts when lost, particularly if there's any other human factors involved."

"Human factors?"

"You mentioned this doctor? What did you call him?"

"The Night Doctor," Eliza said clearly.

"We don't know anything about him or what he wants. If he has anything to do with what's going on, or what's happened to Esme we have to believe he needs her alive as much as we do."

"But the Blade ..." Eliza told him about the Artifact of Arkanos, the shard he had used to transform Alban.

She could hear him typing on the keyboard again. "Arkanos? I see there's an entry in our database from Christopher Wren's original notes. It appears to be a Roman artifact, also referred to as The Healer's Shard, but there isn't much else documented in this particular file. You say it's a blade? Perhaps a scalpel?"

"I don't know," her voice cracked.

There was a long pause. "I'll keep searching and I will call if I can find anything else. I see here that the Order have activated a behavioralist, a search and rescue specialist who's going to be there as soon as he can get to you. He's in Switzerland, so it shouldn't take him long. I already see confirmation that he's received the orders."

"What do I do?"

"Eliza, it's the middle of the night. Get some sleep."

She paused, her mind racing trying to figure out how she could do that. She hadn't had more than a few hours of rest since they left London. Sleep was hard to come by, especially without Faraday to quiet the voices that had haunted her since Dover. He had a way of calming her and charming her into slumber with his warmth and his relaxing purr. Lucky Randall. He had Faraday and Tiberius to cuddle with. She had no one ... and she certainly wasn't cuddling with Phillip Thorpe, arrogant bastard.

"Okay," she finally managed.

Phillip pulled the car into the lot outside the hospital just as the sun bathed the landscape in golden light. Already, a cadre of trucks, utility vehicles, and search teams assembled around the back of one of the trucks. The Incident Commander stood on the tailgate of the vehicle, doling out assignments to the teams. The archeological teams stood nearby, watching. Eliza stood by the car, listening to it all, wondering which one of the search team members might be the behavioralist from Aegis. But her question was answered a moment later when a purple Aro skidded on the gravel driveway at a rate of speed too high for conditions and environment.

Eliza and Phillip jumped out of the path of the vehicle as the driver slammed on his brakes, popped the clutch, put it in park and killed the engine. The older man got out of the car, unfolding his tall, slender frame from the small rental car.

Eliza's breath caught audibly in her throat as he walked around to the boot and popped it open, taking out a backpack and equipment case. Phillip must have heard her, and he nudged her in the ribs. The man looked like James Bond—the Daniel Craig version. He had features chiseled from muscle and experience, bright blue eyes and a head of dark blonde hair, styled in a military crew cut. He wore tactical pants, a white turtle neck and navy blue parka. He pulled on a matching wool cap and closed the boot.

He walked over to the rescue teams and waited patiently to be addressed, standing in a resting military stance. Phillip nudged her again. "Put your tongue back in your mouth, Dr. Wren. You'll catch a fly."

Eliza turned and glared at him, closing her mouth as she realized he was right. "What?" She regained her composure. Phillip ignored her, pressing past her to walk over to the man.

"Dr. Phillip Thorpe," he stuck out his hand. "Aegis Research and Recovery."

The man looked at his hand, lifting his brow, hesitating to accept it. "MacLaren, Boyd MacLaren. Field Commander, North Atlantic SAR Division. Senior Field Operative of the Order. Are you the team lead that lost an Agent?"

His thick Canadian accent reminded Eliza of her father's friend Lionel Cavendish from Regina, Alberta. Now that she knew about the depth of her parent's involvement in the Order, she began to question their associates' involvement as well. Cavendish might have been an Agent too, for all she knew.

"My sister," Eliza said. "It's been almost 24 hours."

"Any Covenant activity in the area?"

"The Covenant?" Eliza gulped. Something about the way he said it made the hair on the nape of her neck prickle. "No. Not recently. At least, not that I am aware of."

"Not that *we* know of," Phillips voice seemed to have dropped half an octave and Eliza thought he looked like he was puffing out his chest to look bigger, more buff. *Competition? Two roosters at odds with one another?*

"If the Covenant is involved, then we have special cause for concern," MacLaren said, his voice remaining low, so as not to interrupt the local authority providing his briefing.

Eliza swallowed hard. "Uh, why?"

"The Covenant doesn't play fair," he said, crisply. "Any game involving *them* is rigged."

"We suspect this may have as much to do with Nazis as the Covenant," Phillip said.

MacLaren's head snapped and his eyes met Phillip's. His brow lifted ever so slowly. "Nazis?"

When the briefing ended, the Canadian operative went to check in with the Incident Commander and asked questions about what efforts had been implemented thus far. He talked to the archeological team that led the search before authorities were called in, and finally came back over to Eliza and Phillip.

"The local authorities will be doing a grid search of the area. They need a personal item from your sister to get her scent."

Eliza went to the car and found Esme's scarf. She took it back over to him. "How long will it take?"

"Hard to say," he said. "I'll give this to the team. They have a drone with a FLIR cam and will be conducting an aerial scan of the area, as well as a search on foot. They'll gradually expand the search, but the terrain is rugged and it may take time. With the weather, though, time is not on our side."

That made Eliza shiver, a squeak escaping her throat. Phillip put a hand on her back to ease her.

"Dr. Wren, how old is your sister?"

"She's not a child," Phillip snapped. "If that's what you're asking."

Boyd MacLaren ignored him. "College educated?"

"She went to art school," Eliza said. "She's twenty-eight."

MacLaren's lips pursed. "Of course she did."

"What's that got to do with anything?" Phillip scowled. "She's missing and her sister is worried sick. Are you here to help or pass judgement?"

"It's not about where she went," MacLaren softened his tone. "It's about knowing the missing person's motivations. Knowing their patterns of behavior and their life experiences that may dictate those patterns. I gave up a ski vacation in San Moritz to be here, so you must understand my only goal is to find your sister and get back to the slopes. The sooner your sister is safely back, the sooner I'm drinking hot toddies in the ski lodge. Understood?"

Eliza nodded. Phillip crossed his arms scowling, but finally capitulated with the raise of a hand and tilt of his head. "So what do we do?" Phillip asked.

"When someone disappears into the wilderness, they leave behind more than just footprints. They leave a trail of behaviors, decisions, and instincts that—when properly understood— can lead us right to them. In this vast, unpredictable wilderness, knowledge of the missing person's behavior is our most reliable compass. Now, who was the last person to see her?"

Phillip hated to admit it, but he raised a hand. "That would be me."

"Uh huh," MacLaren said. "Predictable. So, tell me what happened."

The Canadian Agent squatted down to inspect the ground in the hospital entryway. Footprints were cast in the decades-old layer of dust and detritus atop the terrazzo tiles. "How many people have traipsed through here since Ms. Wren went missing?"

"Eliza and I, primarily," Phillip said. "The rest of the team went around to the tunnel we found behind the building or combed the woods. Eliza and I searched the hospital."

"Are these the shoes you were wearing yesterday?" He directed the questions at both of them, but pointed at Eliza's feet.

"Yes," Eliza said. "It's the only pair I have." Eliza wasn't one of those frilly girls who had closets full of shoes. The one pair of practical leather lace ups were appropriate for every purpose, the office, the lab or the subway. Eliza could borrow her mother's shoes if she had to attend a gala or some fancy event she couldn't avoid. They wore the same size.

"Yes," Phillip said. "I have others, but ..."

MacLaren took a tape measure from the thigh pocket of his tactical pants and pulled it out. "May I, Dr. Wren?" He moved to Eliza. She put a hand on his shoulder and held up her foot. He put the tape to it, paused to inspect it, then nodded. "Thank you." He then did the same to Phillip.

"There are three other sets of tracks in the dust I've observed." He put the tape away. "Dr. Wren, would you say your sister's feet are smaller than yours?"

"No," Eliza said. "Two sizes bigger. Taller than me."

"And how much does she weigh?"

Eliza had to pause to process the question. A lady never wanted to be asked her weight. Esme wasn't overweight—if anything, she was fit, more muscular than Eliza. "Nine and a half stone, maybe."

"What is that in pounds?" Phillip asked.

"60 kilos to pounds ..." MacLaren had the look of a man doing math in his head. "What is that, like 130 pounds?"

"Something like that," Eliza confirmed.

MacLaren nodded, and continued his inspection of the area. "And where was Esme standing the last time you saw her?"

Phillip pointed out the spot, near a long dark hallway that led into a collapsed area of the hospital. "Why do you ask?"

"There was a struggle," he took his torch and shone it on the markings in the dust. "Three tracks. Then, two disappear down the hall. Dr. Wren, you've been down that hall as well."

"Looking for Esme."

"As you would," Boyd allowed. "Does this hallway go to an outside area?"

"There's an exit that goes downstairs and outside, not far from the service entrance to the tunnels," Phillip said. "We've gone as far into the tunnels as we could safely traverse."

"Two people, measuring the size of the prints, it's logical to assume they were male." MacLaren led them down the hallway, following the prints down the stairs and out into the muddy ground behind the hospital. "Here there are only two sets of footprints."

He dropped to one knee, taking out the measuring tape, again. He measured the prints he found in the mud, length and width, then measured the depth. "Puzzling," he said.

"What?" Eliza dropped down beside him.

"The depth of this print suggests a person weighing roughly 81 kilos, or 180 pounds. The pattern of the tread is specific to a Spanish-made boot produced before World War II." He took out his phone and snapped a few pictures. Then, moved to one of the other prints. "This print," he said, taking the tape and measuring it as he had the first. "Is roughly a 195 to 200 pound individual, but there's something interesting about the gait."

"What's that?" Phillip pressed in so he could see.

"If either of them are carrying her sister, then the math is not *mathing*," Boyd stood. "And this second print demonstrates an obvious drag, like someone who walks with a limp." He continued to follow the second track.

"Is that because he's carrying Esme and ... she's too heavy?" Phillip stood, puzzling over the question at hand.

"Unlikely," MacLaren said. "The tracks would have to be much deeper to account for Esme's weight."

"But clearly they continue down into the tunnel," Eliza followed MacLaren like he was her only hope. He was.

"So it would seem," the Canadian operative agreed. "Let's take a look."

15

THE SEARCH AND THE SOLDIER

J ust before 11:00 a.m. Mihai's dark green VW Passat pulled into the car
  lot. Eliza had been pacing for a solid hour, wishing she were out with
the search teams, but talking with the local missing-persons expert seemed
like an equally important task. She hoped he'd be able to convince her that
the scores of missing young men didn't herald a similar end for Esme.

The elderly reporter slung his messenger bag cross-body and extracted
his stiff bones from the car. He moved toward the open-sided tent that
appeared to be the base of operations for the search effort. He had seen
too many of them in his lifetime, never mind how many had been within
five miles of where he found himself now. He spotted Eliza's form and
raised a hand in greeting, then focused on his steps as he crossed the uneven
ground.

One wrong move at his age didn't mean a turned ankle; it meant a
broken hip and months of physical therapy if he was lucky.

Eliza waved back and motioned to someone else Mihai couldn't see. A
tall, dark-haired, scruffy fellow who looked like he belonged in a catalog
advert and a tall woman who looked more Slavic than Balkan joined her

where she stood. They moved together toward him and met him halfway across the car park.

"Good morning, Mr. Corbea," the tall woman said in perfect Romanian with just the slightest hint of a Russian accent. "My name is Irina Popa. I'll be serving as your alternative to a translation app today." She smiled only slightly, no doubt because the circumstances of his visit were so dire.

"That will save a great deal of time," he confirmed. "Who is the man?"

"This is Dr. Phillip Thorpe. He is a member of the archaeological team and is working with Dr. Wren. He was the last person to see Esme."

Eliza's expression soured. She didn't speak Romanian, but hearing the two names in the same sentence was all the translation she needed. Phillip motioned them over to a folding table and chairs under the tent so they could talk.

Eliza took the old man's arm as they walked, supporting his balance as they walked but making it look like he escorted her to the makeshift seating. Mihai was grateful for both.

Irina detailed what they knew about Esme's disappearance, and Eliza watched his expression carefully as he took copious notes in an old-school steno pad. "Is this like ... other disappearances he's heard of in this area?" She desperately hoped he'd shake his head and say they weren't alike at all, but she knew better.

He stroked his bushy mustache for a moment, and then released a flood of melodic words.

"He says that the main difference you already know. Mostly it's men have gone missing in this area, and the only woman he remembers in the last twenty years was a Swiss hiker who got lost with her husband while hiking in the Apuseni Mountains. They were found after maybe sixteen hours. He also said that in a few cases, there was a sign of struggle, but not always. There are many hazards in these mountains. That makes it hard to search."

"What kinds of hazards?" Phillip asked, knowing that would be Eliza's next question, and wanting to spare her voice.

After a flurry of foreign words, "Assuming they even left the hospital grounds, the terrain can be dangerous: there might be sinkholes, ravines, abandoned mine shafts, wild boar, or even bears. Or there may be transients or off-grid residents who are less than welcoming to strangers. The hospital itself presents quite a number of dangers."

Eliza pulled out her phone and began typing. *Would anyone have architectural plans for the hospital? What about maps of mines in the area? Surely those must be filed somewhere.*

Irina translated and Mihai nodded. He reached into his satchel and pulled out photocopies of old floor plans. "He says they have used these before, but they found nothing. About the mines, he will go into town and ask if there are licenses filed. They may have some information there."

A few more questions back and forth revealed that Mihai had little hope to offer, even though he very much wanted to be of assistance. The best thing he could do, they decided, was to get back to Zlatna before the government offices and libraries closed to see what he could find out.

Eliza walked him back to the car in silence. Before he maneuvered himself back into the driver's seat, he took her hand and looked into her eyes. He muttered a few words to her, and though she didn't know the language, she understood the tone. Empathy, even sympathy, from one who had stood in her shoes more times than he cared to count.

She nodded solemnly, tears stinging her eyes again.

She refused to let them fall. She had wept enough. Esme needed her to fight, not grieve.

The day's search was grueling, and the spitty rain which pelted them for nearly forty minutes washed away any hope of finding more footprints.

The grid had expanded to three square kilometers, including mountainous terrain, and checkpoints had been set up every kilometer along the old forestry road that ran through the more remote areas of the grid.

Nothing. They'd found nothing.

The sun bled amber across the treetops as Alpha Team gathered at checkpoint two. Jackets were unzipped, radios clicked to standby, and muddy boots stomped patches of frost into the earth. A thermos of bitter coffee made the rounds.

Phillip stood with Eliza and Boyd at the periphery, listening as the local SAR coordinator, a lean and stern man named Ioan, explained what they'd ruled out.

"We've looked everywhere in the ravines, the streambed, and even the collapsed cistern near the hospital's north wall. There were no drag marks outside the hospital walls, and no prints at all past mid-day yesterday that we were able to find. Now it is all mud and we will not find any more unless they are new."

"You're giving up?" Eliza croaked, her voice raw from trying to call Esme's name during the search. Even with the megaphone Phillip had found for her, her throat hadn't been up to the task.

"We are not giving up, but we need a new strategy. We have a team analyzing the hospital plans, but we have searched everywhere that could be navigated safely. And the footprints seemed to leave the building and head north. We did not find blood, so that is a good thing." He was trying to be reassuring, but the hole Esme's absence left in Eliza's heart couldn't be filled by reassurances.

One of the junior searchers—a young woman with kind eyes and a bright orange scarf—added gently, "It might have been voluntary. People do strange things. Sometimes they just ... walk away."

Eliza's spine stiffened. She tightened her grasp on the emergency whistle around her neck as though it might tether her to sanity. "Walk away?" she repeated, her voice low.

Phillip shot her a warning glance, but she stepped forward anyway.

"She did not ... *walk away.*" A coughing fit overtook her for a moment, and Boyd handed her a bottle of water. She took a sip and then braced herself. It would hurt, but she needed to be heard. "Esme is not some tourist with ... an existential crisis. She was *taken.*"

Ioan held up his hands. "We are not saying she isn't in danger. There were footprints inside which indicate that a scuffle took place." He glared at the junior searcher and she bit her lip, wisely remaining silent.

Another member of the Aegis SAR team, a bearded man with weathered skin and a calm demeanor, chimed in. "Could be a hidden sinkhole. Or maybe an old shaft. We need those maps. Half this forest stands on broken earth."

Boyd nodded. "It's possible. But that wouldn't explain the metaphysical amperage I'm feeling. This place is humming."

The bearded man gave him a look. "With respect, sir, we're just looking for a missing girl. Not ghosts."

That did it.

Eliza stepped in fast, her whispering voice eerily amplified by the megaphone. "She's not missing. She was abducted ... by a man who's spent decades raising the dead. While you're down here prattling on about sinkholes and runaway trauma, he's got her somewhere and he's *using her* for something we probably don't have words for yet!"

The entire clearing fell silent. Even the wind seemed to hold its breath.

Eliza clicked the switch on the megaphone again. "She didn't leave. She's not wandering around waiting to be found. She's being *hidden.* And if we don't stop him ..." She found herself unable to finish the sentence, terrified of what words might have come next.

Boyd cleared his throat. "Well, I think that's our cue to head back and regroup. And come back fresh and blazing tomorrow."

Ioan gave a curt nod, more out of respect than understanding. "We'll keep the night teams going, but if they get a lead—"

"We'll be ready," Phillip said, gently touching Eliza's arm.

Eliza lingered a second longer, staring at the treeline like she could will Esme to reappear. Then she followed.

From above on the hillside, the Watcher studied her as she trudged along behind the others. She represented one of the two turtle doves who had been foretold, he was certain. The other one was nearby—they had no idea that the searchers had come within mere feet of the obscured entrance to the mine.

He felt like he had a front-row seat to a great battle of wits. It was almost as enjoyable as real battle. Almost.

The razor's rim of sunset clung to the hills as the three returned to the farmhouse.

There should be four, Eliza thought, but no words would come, even though Phillip had been decent enough to stop at a local place and pick her up a cup of herbal tea. It wasn't oolong, but it was smooth, and had some sort of mint in it that soothed her vocal folds.

They dragged themselves up the front walk—exhausted, bedraggled, and increasingly desperate.

Eliza entered first, and then Boyd pushed his way through, muttering under his breath. His cargo pants were soaked, and his jacket had lost a button.

"Whole place is like a scrambled compass," he grumbled. "There's a damn magical echo through the trees, but it's like chasing a ghost's shadow down a hall of mirrors."

Phillip closed the door behind him and hung up his coat. "We'll regroup and try again tomorrow. If Esme were here, we might have a way to interpret the signal, but ..." His voice trailed off as he shook his head.

Boyd stomped mud off his boots onto the plastic tray by the door. "If I ever meet this Caspar guy in person, I'm going to feed him one of these trail boots."

Phillip opened his mouth to answer when Alban moved.

The undead soldier, who had been still as a statue in his chair in the corner all day, rose and turned toward the door. He brought his right hand to his forehead and executed a crisp military salute.

Clack, clack.

Boyd's reaction was immediate. He yelped—a short, strangled sound—and stumbled backward into the coatrack, which promptly collapsed under his weight.

"Jesus flipping CHRIST!"

Phillip didn't flinch. He merely inclined his head toward Alban. "At ease."

Boyd pushed himself up, panting slightly. "What the—You captured one? No one told—" The Canadian's arms were tangled in the web of coats as he fumbled to stand. "He's in your *house*? Like he's just *here*?"

Eliza almost smiled.

"He obeys me," Phillip said dryly. "And he's an Order Agent."

"You could give a guy a heart attack, you know that? You didn't think to mention this?"

"I assumed the Order would have briefed you," Phillip countered. "My mind has been on finding Esme." He shot a sideways glance at Eliza to

check her reaction, then turned to Alban. "Have there been any disturbances in our absence?"

Alban blinked once, then shook his head.

"Good man." Phillip moved past him and into the kitchen, where a
SAR map covered the table. "There's something we're missing. There's a
magical field, but it's fractured, splintered, something. Boyd felt it, but he
couldn't triangulate it."

Eliza stepped up behind him, pointing at the mountains just north of
the hospital grounds. "Buried."

Boyd, finally free of the coatrack, leaned in and scanned the notes. "If it's
underground—"

"We really need those mine maps," Phillip finished. "And spelunking
gear."

16

WHAT BINDS THE UNIVERSE

Eliza paced the length of the folding table beneath the tent, fuming. Her eyes burned more from anger than from grief, though both fueled her at the moment. Teams were already out searching in the freezing rain. Operational search dogs barks in the distance. Phillip and Boyd had gone with one of the teams to search an abandoned factory the drone had picked up on the day before. Eliza waited for Mihai to return with the diagrams of the mines.

Phillip had expressly forbidden anyone from entering the mines until this data was available due to the inherent hazards of the confined spaces, with possible unguarded mineshafts, and inevitable dead ends. Eliza seriously considered ignoring his orders, but she wasn't sure where the entrances to the mines were. There might be more than one. Maybe she could find them, but it was a dangerous undertaking. Besides, he wasn't her boss. Which reminded her, she hadn't heard back from Randall since she'd called him in the middle of the night.

She took out her phone and dialed the number, putting it to the speaker. Randall answered without his customary greeting. "Save your voice, Eliza.

I have something to tell you." He didn't wait for her to ask. "I was just confirming my findings before I called. I think I'm there." He took a breath, and she could hear his chair squeak as he sat down and pulled up his computer.

"I found a book in the British Library called *The Chronicles of Arkanos*," he said, the keys chattering as he typed. "An archivist wrote it to preserve the history of Thrace before the Nazis wiped out anyone who might remember. The onslaught wasn't as bad as they feared, but the war did take a tremendous toll on everyone in the area. At one time, according to the archivist, it was a Roman settlement. In the time of the Roman Empire, an occult healer, Arkanos of Thracia served both a battlefield physician, a devotee of the god of medicine Aesculapius, and a *mágos*—a mage. He forged two sacred blades, and imbued them with the power of a meteorite. He meant it to conquer death. This angered Pluto."

"God of the Underworld?" Eliza managed.

"Exactly," Randall agreed. "One was meant to heal, the other meant to kill. Arkanos wielded both. While the dagger could open the veil between life and death, the scalpel was meant to close it, to keep the patient on *this* side of the veil."

"Dichotomy," Eliza observed.

"More of a paradox, actually." He paused. "The data I've been able to track down about the blades suggests there is a resonance between them."

"If this Night Doctor ... has the scalpel," Eliza spoke softly, her voice heavy and hoarse from the previous day's hunt. "Where is the dagger?"

"Intel suggests the blades traveled between a series of antiquities dealers through Spain, which may be how this Dr. Caspar Escaverra, or the Night Doctor, got a hold of the scalpel. But the Covenant found the dagger. An unknown source reported it was last owned by the High Seer of the Obsidian Covenant."

The silence crashed down around them. The screaming in Eliza's brain took over everything. Her heart thundered into her throat and she felt light-headed. "*M-M-Maelis.*" The name trembled on her lips.

"I'm afraid so," he said. "Which makes it all the more urgent that we find this artifact and secure it before the Covenant does. Imagine the power they could wield with both fragments? Imagine the power of a weapon that has touched both death and resurrection?"

"You mean ... me," Eliza said.

"That may be why it threatened you specifically, Eliza. That's why you must stay as far away from the artifact, the scalpel, as you can. You're fragile enough as it is, but ... dear girl ... you are particularly vulnerable to this Blade. Your blood is the key to its hunger. It knows you are near, and it will stop at nothing to have you."

Eliza shivered, too numb to imagine the possibilities that faced her.

"There is an inscription in the book that I have translators working on. It says, *Lama tânjește după viața care a gustat moartea.*"

"Sounds Romanian," she commented.

"Perhaps," Randall allowed.

"I have a translator. Text it to me," she said, then hesitated before saying, "Thank you, Randall. Truly."

"Eliza, I don't have to tell you how important it is that you stay as far away from that Blade as ..." she didn't want to think about the threat, and she reached up and disconnected the call.

Irina arrived just as Mihai pulled into the lot. A thin layer of ice coated his car, and the temperatures were dropping. Winter weather was a real possibility in the overnight hours. The reporter carried a box overflowing with aging paper scrolls that were too large for the box. Eliza rushed to help him, catching a couple of the blue prints before they hit the wet ground.

"Are these the maps?" Eliza asked. Irina translated.

"Da, da," Mihai nodded, pulling his coat around his neck.

"Yes," she said. "These are the maps the rescue team asked for."

"Before we start," Eliza said, opening her text messages from Randall. "What does this say?"

Irina took her phone and gazed at the message. Mihai moved closer so he could see it. They both exchanged a cautious glance. Irina handed the phone back to Eliza. "It says *the blade longs for a life that has tasted death*," she said.

"Oh," Eliza sat back down, gutted.

It was midday when Phillip and Boyd returned to base, pleased to discover the maps had arrived. Boyd radioed the local Incident Commander and let him know they needed to come back to base. But it took time. The teams had all morning to get deeper into the woods, expanding the search grid to spots they hadn't gotten to the day before.

In the meantime, Mihai had coordinated with the café in town and had brought boxed lunches for the search teams. There were cardboard containers with plastic liners full of coffee and tea, as well as bottled water and other snacks and beverages. It was difficult feeding an army of searchers in such a remote area, but Mihai volunteered to assist, and Eliza was grateful for it.

She wasn't particularly hungry, but Phillip and Boyd both offered to bring her a sandwich, or get her a beverage. She finally acquiesced when Phillip just brought her a box containing a sandwich, a plastic bag containing fresh green onions, sliced tomatoes, cucumbers, carrot sticks, and a bag of potato crisps. She wasn't sure what type of sandwich she at first, but Irina identified it as a roasted eggplant salad sandwich, and while she didn't have the emotional desire to eat, her stomach growled and she forced the food down.

The Incident Commander arrived as she sat nibbling on crisps, scanning the maps trying to make sense of it all. Irina pointed out the different icons on the legend, explaining what they stood for. As an engineer, Eliza wasn't unaccustomed to reading schematics, and noted where exhaust vents were located, electrical rooms, and the elevator shafts.

Irina explained that the coal mine here was one of the largest in Romania. "The mine has reserves of 39.3 million tonnes of coal."

"Not active?"

Irina shrugged, sitting back in her chair. "There were several fatal accidents in 1998 and while they tried to address the safety issues, the government ordered a cease and desist nearly a decade later."

"So, it's ... unsafe." It wasn't a question.

Irina shook her head. "Twelve miners died in the last incident. Four of the deceased were would-be rescuers."

"What happened?"

"There was a fire," she said. "Lignite is a highly combustible variety of coal. It's often referred to as brown coal."

"Carbon content?" Eliza asked.

"It's 25-35%," Irina sat forward, clearly recognizing Eliza's expertise in chemistry. "I worked here just out of college, and an intern, before I joined the Order. Brown coal is considered the lowest rank of coal due to its relatively low heat content. It's got a high moisture content, so it produces less heat for the amount of carbon dioxide and sulfur, compared to other forms of coal. It was once highly prized for running steam engines, but now it's almost exclusively used in steam-electric power generation."

"How hot?"

"Hot enough to be fatal," she said. "ten to twenty megajouls per kilogram." She reached for a notebook and pulled it over, flipping it open to a blank page. She began sketching out a partial molecular structure, showing the hydrocarbon configuration creating a benzene ring.

Eliza's finger hovered over the diagram, a thousand questions raced through her mind. "Toxic?"

"Yes," Irina said. "Respiratory inhalation is the greatest hazard, but renal failure, hepatocellular necrosis are the worst of it. Skin and eye irritation can be highly problematic."

"Black lung?"

"Commonly seen in this region, though the locals commonly refer to it as *brown lung*."

Eliza glanced up realizing Boyd and Phillip were listening intently. MacLaren's sandwich hung limp in his hand. Phillip had a crisp halfway to his mouth and froze as he processed the real dangers in the mines.

"We're going to need some additional protective equipment," Boyd dropped his sandwich and pulled out his phone, typing out a text message.

No. No! Eliza wanted to scream. Esme didn't have time for protective equipment! The clock was ticking! That maniac might have already killed her. A morbid vision of Esme in a similar state as Alban flashed behind her eyes and filled her with dread.

Clack! Clack! Clack! Eliza could hear Esme's teeth rattling together.

"Alban!" Eliza stood, abruptly snapping out of her vision. " He doesn't need protective equipment." Her throat burned like fire, but she forced the words past the eternal lump in her larynx. "He can go find Esme. He knows her. She has a ... connection with him. She can ... call out to him. We need Alban ... here. Now."

"Eliza," Phillip caught her by the arm, clearly alarmed by her outburst. He drew her into him, trying to soothe her. "I know you're scared. This is a very scary situation, but honey. You need to keep a level head. Alban isn't a bloodhound that we can turn loose to go and find her. He isn't Lassie and Esme isn't *Timmy in the well*."

Eliza shoved him and pulled away in the same movement. "What?" She glared. "She's my ... sister. We have to find her ... we have ... to..." waves of coughing washed over her and she buckled, falling to her knees with the uncontrollable wheezing and gasping for air, her throat pressed past its limits.

Phillip glanced up at Boyd and the two shared a questioning glance. "He does see you as his commanding officer ..." Boyd said. "You could give the order."

Phillip's face twisted in disbelief that the Canadian behaviorist might even consider something so ridiculous. He scooped up Eliza and helped her to the car. "When did you last sleep?"

Eliza was in no condition to answer.

Back at the farmhouse, Eliza sat at the table with a cup of tea in her hands. Out of the cold, and properly lubricated with honey and lemon, her throat felt better, but her resolve had not lessened. Alban stood at the end of the table. "Listen up, soldier," Phillip spoke in a commanding voice. "A comrade is missing, and you may be the only one who can find her. Do you remember Esme?"

Alban, standing at attention, gazed forward, unblinking. Not even a chatter of his teeth.

"Can you find her?" Eliza asked, desperate for any sign of recognition. *Nothing.*

"What about the Night Doctor?" Phillip asked. "Can you sense him? Could you find your way back to him?"

Nothing.

A cry broke from Eliza's throat, her heart breaking. "He doesn't ... remember."

Alban was her last hope. Boyd had ordered the appropriate equipment expedited to the site, but another night without her sister safely returned was another night she wouldn't sleep. She didn't know how much longer she could continue.

"Wait," Eliza said, standing from her chair. "Where's his control object?"

Phillip did a double take. "His what?"

"The dog tags. Maybe that's it," Eliza said. "His connection. To ... the doctor. If he's taken Esme, or ... or knows where she is, maybe we can use that link to find her. "

Eliza convinced Phillip to bring Alban and his dogtags to the site. There was no use putting the tags back if it meant they lost control of him before they were ready. Phillip stood chewing on his thumbnail, arms crossed, panic hidden just beneath the surface of his ragged face. He hadn't shaved in days, a rugged rafe that didn't match his scholarly personality. Eliza held a box knife, the only implement she could find to accomplish the task at hand. Alban lay still on the folding table inside the tent, as ordered. She peeled back his t-shirt and found the void where the dogtags once rested. "It's still open," Eliza said.

"I tried stitching him up, but the skin is so desiccated the threads tore through it like paper. It's strange. His dislocated arm healed, but this incision didn't."

Eliza stepped back, putting down the knife she didn't need. She paced a moment, considering her options. "Alban, stay here, I'll be right back."

She disappeared, leaving Phillip looking stunned. When she returned with a roll of silver duct tape, his expression didn't change. "Duct tape?"

"It binds the universe," Eliza said. "An engineer's best friend when things go off the rails."

"Do you know what the difference between a mechanical engineer and civil engineer is?" Phillip asked, out of the blue, clearly finding a need to fill the void of silence.

Eliza glanced over at him, cocking a brow as if to ask, *what?*

"Mechanical engineers build weapons," Phillip said. "Civil engineers build targets."

"The definition of ... an engineer is," Eliza retorted, "someone who makes precision guesswork ... based on unreliable data ... provided by people with questionable ... knowledge. Never wrong. Likes tables."

Phillip realized then that she'd gotten his joke and come back with one better, despite the strain on her voice. A hearty laugh erupted from his chest, breaking the tension of the moment.

MacLaren pulled back the canvas tent flap and entered, his eyes narrowing when he spotted Alban lying on the table. The levity in the tent blew away like snowflakes.

Clack. Clack. Clack. Clack.

"What the hell is *he* doing here?" MacLaren demanded. "It's almost dark," he said to Phillip. "What are you doing back here?"

"Alban doesn't need daylight ... to search for Esme," Eliza said. "Besides, the ... mines are dark too, right?"

Boyd hesitated a moment. "The crews have called it for the day."

"We haven't," Phillip said. "We're going in."

Boyd looked like he might protest, and rubbed his chin in exasperation. "How much training have you had on respiratory protection and confined space entry?"

"Mandatory training ... even for rookies," Eliza snapped.

"Good." Boyd walked over to a box on the table. "The equipment I ordered just arrived."

"Let's gear up then," Phillip said, having to rush over and grab Alban who shuffled toward the exit of the tent. "Not yet, soldier."

He handed Eliza an N-95 half face respirator designed for dust particles. "Look, federal regulators don't require respirators as a primary means of protection for coal dust."

"Protective equipment ... always the last line ... of defense," Eliza said.

"What do you mean?" Phillip asked.

"Engineering controls are always the first order of business when controlling hazards," Boyd said. "Controlling the dust is a primary requirement, but since this mine hasn't been operational we don't know what the conditions are. It might not be dusty at all. Equipment may not be operational. I recommend keeping these on at all times. Only intrinsically safe equipment. I have flashlights and a four-gas meter to monitor the oxygen and flammable gas levels and will test periodically as we traverse the mine."

Alban started for the tent flap, as if something were drawing him away. "Not yet, Alban." Phillip caught him this time, and held him back.

"If I tell you to get out, don't argue. Don't hesitate, turn around and run back the way we came. Most of the hazards down there can take you out in seconds, and this dust mask will not protect you from oxygen deficiency."

"Noted," Eliza said.

"Phillip, you'll need to shave. You need a good seal," Boyd ordered.

Phillip's hand went to his jaw, realizing how scruffy he'd gotten. "Got a razor?"

"As a matter of fact," Boyd said, pulling his Bowie knife from the sheath on his hip. "I do."

"Now that's a proper field shave," Boyd chortled, surveying the raw skin on Phillip's chin.

"Yeah, very funny. But we're wasting time. Eliza, are you ready?"

She nodded and held up a four-inch length of duct tape in one hand and Alban's tags in the other.

Phillip's eyes widened and he stepped back, watching her replace the dog tags, then tape the skin—what was left of it—closed, leaving the chain hanging from the wound like a rip cord, just in case this didn't work. She pulled down Alban's worn t-shirt and set the tape aside. "Now we wait."

Alban twitched, his eyes going from cloudy to pitch black, and back to cloudy. One minute he lay still, the next he had his hands around Phillip's throat, his teeth clattering feverishly.

"Alban! No!" Eliza cried in a ragged breath. "No!"

Boyd rammed into Alban's side with his shoulder, a rugby move, and sent Alban careening off to the far side of the tent. Phillip doubled over, clutching his throat and gasping. "That ... didn't take ... long," he wheezed.

Clack. clack. clack.

Alban turned, moving more quickly than his usual shuffling gait, made for the half-open tent flap, but Boyd moved faster. He caught the bone-thin arm of the Awakened, and examined him. Alban protested, as much as the undead being could, his teeth chattering frantically. It was an effort to keep him subdued, but Boyd caught him in a bear hug and held him fast.

"Well, kids, this dog is ready to hunt. Grab the gear and let's get going!"

17

HUNGER

Even though she still wore Caspar's coat, Esme shivered against the cold stone floor. She strained against the bits of wire binding her to the girder, but not enough to injure her wrists. Eliza's voice echoed through her mind, warning her about tetanus. Her shots were up-to-date, of course, but she'd spent a lifetime of her absent-minded abandon being curbed by the practicality of her sister's voice.

The thought of Eliza tightened her chest. Tetanus or no, her sister would want her to fight to get free. Even if she got her hands free, though, Esteban stood like a sentinel just a few feet away, with orders to keep an eye on her and not let her escape. She could barely see his outline in the doorway, since Caspar had taken the lantern to another chamber with him.

The darkness suffocated her, but she couldn't stop herself from studying the different shades of black, naming each of them in her artist's brain: *nyx, midnight coal, night's secret.*

"Esteban?" Esme whispered, hoping that even in his controlled state, he might respond to her if watching her was his mission. "Esteban, can you hear me?"

He didn't react. She hadn't expected him to. His silence was absolute, and the static that came from his mind was like listening to a microwave reheat a plate of soggy chips.

Beneath that, though, the electric crackle of the Blade's energy prickled against Esme's consciousness. It knew Eliza would come for her. Esme feared what would happen then, but she hoped she'd survive long enough to warn Eliza of the depth of the danger.

The distant wavering of the lantern's light drew her from her fearful thoughts. Caspar drew near.

"I apologize for leaving you so long," the Night Doctor said amiably, as if he didn't have her trussed to a girder. "I was preparing. You will see. And it is my hope that we can find some way for you to be useful. Esteban, please hold her still."

Her Awakened guard shuffled over and gripped her upper arms with surprising strength. If she made it out of here, she would be bruised. She wondered what colors the bruises would be and how they might look against the shades of black she'd filed away earlier.

Caspar stepped behind her and carefully untwisted the bits of wire that bound her. She felt blood rush into her hands, but without the wetness that would accompany a wound. Eliza would be pleased.

Esme considered the color red and how roses and blood could be the same hue.

Esteban's firm hands pulled Esme to her feet.

"Well done, *mi hijo*," Caspar praised him. "Bring her." Caspar strode out of the chamber and Esteban turned to follow, forcing Esme to walk backwards. When they stopped moving, she found herself in the chamber where she had first awakened.

Caspar had been busy with the chalk, tracing Latin phrases and a variety of sigils Esme didn't recognize on the stone walls, the wooden doorframe, and even the floor.

"The Blade seeks a sacrifice, I'm afraid. Pluto wishes for it to be your sister, I think. But perhaps there is still another way." Caspar reached into the brass bowl and drew forth the Blade. The lantern's glow did not glint off the darkened metal; rather, the instrument seemed to create a hole in the light. Esme found herself surprised by how much it looked like the combination of a modern scalpel and the palette knife she used in her studio. In his hand, though, it filled her with terror. "You—you could still save us all. Just speak to him. Speak to Esteban."

He turned toward her holding the Blade in front of him as she would hold a paintbrush. Despite the calm of his tone, there was madness in his eyes.

Survive. Eliza's voice rippled through her consciousness. *Survive at any cost.*

She had only one chance to avoid the Awakened's fate.

"I—I've had an idea," she muttered weakly, still unsure if she should give up the secret she held. "I think I know why Alban is different."

Caspar's eyes shifted to his son, then back to her with a fearful intensity. "Tell me."

She had no choice. It was her only leverage. Her only chance. "When we first found Alban, he had his dog tags sewn into his side."

"Yes, this must be done to keep the Awakened from becoming wild and unpredictable."

"So Esteban has such an item?"

"He does. I removed it when I first discovered it, but he became ... unstable. The Nazis would have destroyed him instantly. So I put it back."

"You must remove it." It was a gamble, Esme knew. Esteban may well become a danger rather than a good soldier like Alban. "It is blocking his mind from me, I think."

Caspar considered her. "If this is a trick, I will cut your throat and you will join my sons."

"It isn't a trick. I just don't want to be sacrificed to some crusty Roman deity."

"That is a powerful motivation. But I am not a fool." He left the chamber, only to return moments later with another of his Awakened.

The new one's appearance shocked her. Unlike Alban and Esteban, this one's skin retained a beige tint rather than grey. His expression was as blank as Esteban's, his foggy eyes as empty, but long strands of dark hair hung limp against his neck. He looked less like a mummy and more like a sick human. He was more newly made, Esme theorized.

"Antonio, take Esteban's place holding the girl. Esteban, come stand beside me." Both of the undead men followed Caspar's orders to the letter. "And now we shall see if you tell the truth or seek to deceive me."

He turned Esteban so that the dark scar on his left side faced the pale LED light. Then Caspar set the Blade down and pulled a small pen knife out of his pocket. He leaned down and probed Esteban's side carefully, then made a small incision near the scar. Esteban didn't flinch. Then Caspar inserted the knife and pulled out a ring.

The reaction was immediate. Esteban's eyes flashed black for an instant, then he threw his head back, his mouth open in a near-silent scream.

What wasn't silent was the torrent of images, incomplete thoughts, and mangled emotions that crashed into Esme's brain. She cried out and her knees buckled. She would have collapsed into a heap on the floor, had Antonio not been holding her in place. Wave after wave of nonsensical psychic data battered her mind. All her other senses fell away, and there remained only the maelstrom inside her.

It wasn't like Alban. Not at all. But it must work the same way, mustn't it? Esme tried to hush the chaos. *Esteban!* She threw his name into the mental squall like a lifeline. *Esteban! Calm down! Let me help you!*

She sensed a ripple of awareness, and the mental storm quieted, though it still lacked order or direction.

"Esteban," she moaned, and the strangled sound of her own voice brought back her ability to hear and see.

"My son! My son!" Caspar, weeping, had dropped the pocket knife and gripped Esteban's hands in his own.

"He doesn't understand what's happening," Esme told the doctor. Pictures flashed in Esme's mind—memories that weren't hers.

A woman stands by the kitchen counter, the chop-chop-chop of her knife counting a cadence on the cutting board, the scent of onions and garlic cooking filling the air.

An azure sky, puffy clouds floating past, as the soft sound of waves lapping the side of the boat sang an afternoon lullaby.

He adjusts the dial on the binoculars, straining to make out the names of the boats floating in the distance in the bay.

These were Esteban's memories, floating past her like dandelion fluff, untethered and following the flow of the breeze. "He remembers his life a little," Esme offered, "but he can't make sense of it. He doesn't know how to use my mind to create order."

The father's weeping gave way to unrestrained tears, and Caspar found himself quite unable to reply.

Esteban couldn't think, not clearly. He could only *feel*, and he was confused and afraid. If he remembered any of the past 80 years, Esme sensed no sign of it. She wondered if he could feel her the way she could feel him.

The woods were unnaturally quiet.

Corporal Alban Wren moved through the forest with a singular purpose—like a homing pigeon returning to its master. He trudged along with mechanical precision, his feet dragging ever-so-slightly through the undergrowth and moss.

Eliza, Phillip, and Boyd kept close behind him, eyes fixed on the undead soldier's back. A few centimeters of the bead chain attached to the dogtags dangled from the edge of the duct tape along his ribs, and Eliza couldn't help feeling that they'd somehow betrayed him.

"He's not ... in there anymore, is he?" she whispered.

Phillip, walking just behind her, shook his head. "The Doctor's influence is fully in control now. Or the Blade's. I guess we aren't sure. The signal is like ... a beacon, I guess."

"Or a leash," Boyd muttered from the rear, brushing pine boughs aside. "I don't like the idea of leashing a soldier."

"He would have volunteered if he could," Phillip offered, trying to ease their consciences.

The wind stirred overhead, ruffling the canopy in the fading light. "We're getting close," Boyd added, his voice low. "There's a different resonance in this part of the woods. Like we're walking through a high-pressure system."

The trees thinned, giving way to a sloping embankment choked with brambles and slick stone. Alban moved on unbothered.

Phillip stumbled and grabbed a tree trunk to catch his balance. "This isn't even a proper game trail. I don't know how Alban isn't going ass over elbow." Eliza grunted in agreement.

Boyd scanned the terrain. "This trail wasn't meant to be found. If it's a mine he's leading us to, and I'll just bet it is, they're often sealed and buried."

Alban came to a halt.

Before them, half hidden by a patch of wild laurel, yawned a dark cleft in the earth. Boyd reached into his pack and passed an intrinsically-safe headlamp to Eliza, then Phillip.

"This is it." Eliza's heart thundered against her ribcage. *Hang in there, Esme. I'm coming.*

Alban raised one bony hand and laid it on the stone, then stepped into the crevice. The darkness swallowed him and he disappeared from view.

Boyd surged forward. "We can't let him out of sight. It could be a labyrinth down there." He flicked on his headlamp and drew a machete from a sheath along his thigh. "For the record, if his head turns 180 degrees or he starts shrieking in Latin, I'm not calling for a team huddle."

No one replied. They didn't need to.

They followed the dead man into the mine.

Esme, still held fast by Antonio, watched Esteban wander aimlessly around the chamber. Another of the Awakened—Francisco, the doctor had called him—blocked the doorway so that Esteban couldn't wander off into the depths of the mine.

"Things will be different now. You will tell me how Esteban responds to the ritual. This is how we will save them!" Caspar's eyes gleamed with a wild combination of hope and madness. He set a rickety crate in the center of the room and set the brass bowl of chalk on top with the Blade across it. His voice rose as he intoned a Latin invocation:

"Pluto, Deus Inferorum, Pater Umbrae,

Accipe hanc hostiam, non vivam nec mortuam.

Per sanguinem et silentium, nos tibi servimus.

Aperi portas Orci, et audi preces meas.

Redde animam ex tenebris, et vincula solve."

His eyes fluttered to Esme, and he repeated his prayer in English, in hopes that her understanding would finally unlock the mystery of restoring the Awakened to the lives they had been denied:

"Pluto, God of the Underworld, Father of Shadows,

Receive this offering, neither living nor dead.

Through blood and silence, we serve you.

Open the gates of Orcus, and heed my plea.

Return the soul from darkness, and break its chains."

He lifted the Blade from the would-be altar and drew it lightly across his own forearm. Blood welled from the wound and dripped crimson onto the chalkdust. The Blade hummed, and Esme whimpered, unable to tune out the deafening din. The sigils on the wall began to glow and pulse a deep orange.

A strangled cry escaped Caspar's lips and Esteban froze in place. "At last! I knew you were the key! Antonio, bring her!"

The Awakened man followed the orders, and Esteban watched as Esme struggled in terror. She felt the tendrils of his awareness—*thought* would be too generous a term—prickling, probing the bond between them. He still didn't know what was happening, but he knew she was his anchor. He knew she was in danger, even if he didn't understand why.

The Blade's hum rose to a fever pitch and the *others* filed into the chamber and positioned themselves along the wall, summoned to the ritual space by the relic's mystical resonance.

"Hold her arm out," Caspar's eyes went wild, his face contorting into a mask of madness. Esteban stepped forward, watching closely as Francisco stepped away from the door and stepped up behind Esme, snaking his withered arm around her to restrain her so that Antonio could use both his hands to force her arm into position.

Caspar turned his gaze to his son. "Here, *mi hijo*, mingle her blood with mine. This is what Pluto asks of us. This is the price of your freedom." He slipped the Blade into Esteban's hand.

"Esteban," Esme pleaded. "You don't have to do this. You don't *want* to do this!" She reached out with her mind, but it was like wading through quicksand.

The first of the Awakened sons gripped the Blade, but hesitated, looking back and forth from Esme to his father. *Papá.* Esme felt the recognition as Esteban looked at the crazed man before him. He still couldn't put the building blocks of coherence together, but he knew that his father was hurting the girl who left footprints in the disorder of his Awakened mind.

In a sudden flash, the glow from the sigils intensified, giving the appearance of burning magma etched into the walls. Heat radiated from the markings.

"Yes!" Caspar cried. He wrapped his fingers around Esteban's to help his son make the incision, but when his forefinger contacted the ancient bronze, his eyes widened. "She has come! Alban has brought her to us!" He grinned at Esme. "Your blood is the key, but *hers* is a sacrifice worthy of a god!"

Esteban stared at his father, then turned to Esme. She pushed the bond toward him, pleading through the spiritual cord between them. He blinked, not because he needed to, but because he *felt.*

No. Wrong. Bad.

Movement at the door drew Esme's eye, and Alban ambled in, his eyes empty and hollow. She let out a wail of grief and fear. She reached out to him, but her mind found only the empty blankness of the Awakened.

He shuffled forward and then stood quiet, having achieved his goal of returning to the Night Doctor's side.

"Liza, RUN!" Esme screamed, hoping her sister would hear her and stay far away from the Blade that thirsted for her blood.

Caspar tightened his grip on the Blade. "She will not run. You see? Everything is—"

"Get away from her!" Eliza's brittle voice cut through the chamber.

She, Phillip, and Boyd rushed into the chamber and froze at the sight of the gathering of Awakened sons.

"You cannot stop me. Pluto demands this in exchange for the return of their souls!" Caspar lifted the Blade, still clutched in Esteban's hand, its darkened bronze glinting in the lava-toned light radiating from the walls.

"Esteban, please," Esme whimpered, and a spark flickered in his eyes. He resisted his father's downstroke, and the delay gave Eliza the opening she needed.

She couldn't make it to Esme's side, not with all the Awakened around them, but she didn't have to. She lunged forward and grabbed the bead chain, ripping the dogtags out of Alban's taped-up wound.

His head jerked back, his mouth open. *Freedom!* The Blade's hold over him snapped like a brittle thread.

Caspar wrenched the Blade out of Esteban's hesitant fingers. The relic's influence engulfed him, and he lurched toward Eliza, Pluto's ultimate prize. The Night Doctor dove forward, his instrument aimed at Eliza's heart.

But Alban stepped between them.

The Blade plunged deeply.

There was a pause. A silence.

Alban gazed at Esme. *Thank you, child of my blood. I am free.*

He exhaled once, a smile of triumph and peace crossing his face. A tiny light escaped from the wound, like a spectral will o'the wisp, and then the soldier's body crumpled into a pile of dust and bone.

And then, mayhem.

The Awakened surged toward Phillip, Boyd, and Eliza, Caspar and the Blade's unspoken command to *DEFEND!* dictating their actions. Desiccated limbs flew as Boyd wielded his machete, but the undead felt no pain and kept coming. Antonio and Francisco still held Esme, placing the odds at five against three.

"The god will not be denied," Caspar hissed, all semblance of the human doctor he had been melting away under the Blade's influence. He began to lift the Blade again, this time targeting Esme.

But Esteban moved forward, some semblance of his own will driving him. *NO. NO, PAPÁ.* He wrapped his arms around his father holding him tight, pinning the Night Doctor's arms. *WRONG.*

Caspar struggled violently against his son's grip. He gripped the blade tightly, fighting to free his arm and use the scalpel, not as the instrument of healing it should have been, but as an instrument of sacrifice. *"Mi hijo, you don't understand. I must—"* He twisted his torso, but Esteban held fast, sliding his capturing embrace lower on his father's arms, forcing the blade downward. Caspar's words were cut short as the Artifact of Arkanos sunk into the flesh of his own thigh.

Everything stopped.

The Awakened ceased their attacks.

Esme held her breath.

Even the dust in the air hung in suspension.

Caspar gasped.

And then—his body began to decay.

The years crashed over him like a wave. Hair greyed. Skin shriveled. Flesh flaked away from bone like dried paper.

He turned his eyes to his son in his final act, and the boy laid his head gently against his father's shoulder, releasing the grip that had stayed the Doctor's hand.

Caspar's remains collapsed in a heap, the Blade clattering to the floor beside him. Esteban sat beside the withered husk of his father.

One by one, wisps rose from each of the Awakened, their remains crumbling to the ground in grey piles. Esteban, the first of the Awakened sons, was the last. He turned his eyes to Esme. *Gracias.* And then he, too, crumbled to ash.

No longer bound, Esme rushed forward and threw her arms around her sister. The two of them wept shamelessly in relief. Phillip turned away to hide his own tears at the relief of their reunion.

"Well." Boyd pulled a containment baggie from his pack and turned it inside out over his hand, using it as a glove to pick up the Artifact. He wrapped the bag around it as he walked back toward the doorway. "That happened."

He zippered the containment bag shut, choking off the Blade's magic. The dust piles that had been the Awakened crackled and began to spark.

Boyd's eyes widened. "Time to go!" he ordered, shoving the sisters, still clinging to each other, out the doorway and into the main shaft. "NOW! MOVE!"

Eliza grabbed Esme's arm and began to run back the way they'd come. Phillip and Boyd raced along behind them. The first *pop* from within the mine was followed by a deep rumble, and Eliza dug deep, knowing they needed to move *faster*. The earth trembled as the coal dust began to ignite in the shaft behind them.

The four of them bolted up the tunnel, their feet pounding against the crumbling rock. Behind them, the ritual chamber was engulfed in a *whoosh* of flame from the piles of the Awakened's dust, each pyre igniting the next.

Esme's hand locked in Eliza's, slick with sweat and dirt. Boyd followed, the containment bag holding the Blade clutched tightly in his arms. Phillip brought up the rear.

Whump! A low percussive wave rippled the walls of the mine like a growl in the mountain's gut.

The tunnels groaned. Wood supports snapped like twigs under the immense weight. Heat rose from the depths of the shaft.

A second detonation boomed below—closer this time. The tunnel floor lurched, throwing them forward. Rocks slammed into their backs.

"Go! Go! GO!" Boyd roared.

Ahead, the mine shaft's mouth flickered with twilight, a jagged wound in the earth granting them passage back to the forest.

The air was thick now, choked with smoke and dust. The walls vibrated with the fury of the collapsing tunnels. A burst of superheated wind tore past them, yanking ash and sparking embers into their faces.

They burst from the entrance just as the mine behind them exploded in a thunderous roar.

A ball of flame chased them, licked at their heels—then collapsed inward as the tunnel imploded, burying itself in its own wrath.

The blast hurled them onto the mossy ground outside, a black plume rising skyward as the forest shuddered.

Esme lay flat on her back, looking up at the stars peeking through the canopy of trees overhead. Her lungs were ragged, her heart hammering.

Eliza rolled over behind her, coughing. "You good?"

"Not even close," Esme gasped. "But I'm alive."

Boyd groaned from somewhere nearby. "I *hate* mines. I *hate* necromancy. I need a drink the size of a canoe."

"I'm buying," Phillip sputtered.

"Eliza." Esme reached for her sister's hand and squeezed it. "No more tunnels."

"Deal," Eliza croaked, squeezing back.

EPILOGUE

ALL THAT REMAINS

B ack at the Incident Command post, Boyd placed the Blade inside the silver case labeled with the Aegis seal and the words *Artifact Containment Kit* stenciled on the top. He closed it and activated an electronic locking mechanism. A *whoosh* erupted from inside like a vacuum seal.

Meanwhile, Phillip completed his triage on Esme. She had lacerations, a few minor burns and contusions. Her wrists were bruised from the restraints, but all in all it wasn't as bad as it could have been. Esme rose from the chair and held it for her sister, but stayed close and accepted the bottle of water Boyd offered. Phillip tended to Eliza next.

"Okay?" MacLaren asked.

"Yeah," Esme said, though she wasn't entirely certain. "I will be." Her hand went to the bandage on her arm. She turned to her sister. "Eliza? Are you okay?"

"I'm fine," she pushed Phillip's hand away as he reached for a lock of hair, intending to brush the loose strand off her forehead. "I'm fine." She repeated to him, glaring at him fiercely.

"So what happens to the Artifact now?" Esme asked Boyd as he pulled a chair over, sitting down beside her. The Incident Command tent was empty, and with the canvas flaps closed, it shielded them from the cold wind that came down between the mountains.

"That's above my paygrade," Boyd said. "It'll be secured, of course. But how? That's not for me to decide."

Esme turned to Phillip. "Will you come back with us to London?"

Phillip glanced at Eliza who stood and turned her back on him as she walked over to the table where snacks and drinks sat for the rescue crews. "London? No." he took the chair Eliza had vacated. "No. My place is here. With the archaeological team."

"What's left to do, eh?" Boyd asked. "You've got the Artifact of Arkanos. Surely you're not thinking you'll find something better than that under that rickety old hospital?"

"There's still work to do here." Phillip's glance passed between Esme and Boyd, surprised by the question. "Surely you can understand, the secret to discovery isn't just in the finding. It's in the search. That's what truly matters. And the search is never done."

Eliza glanced back at him, her braid falling from her shoulder. Something in her expression seemed to catch him off guard. She made a quick retreat out the tent flap. Outside, the wind struck her in her face and the season's first snow fell in swirling ribbons of sparkles illuminated by a near full moon that peered from the banks of clouds that swirled over the mountains.

A mixture of feelings flooded her mind. Relief for her sister's safety. Grief for Alban. Even pity for the Night Doctor. Caspar had been every bit a victim of the Blade, as had the Awakened. The Nazis had used Caspar and his sons for their own maniacal gains. And ironically, they had gained nothing.

It was all so futile. She wanted to scream. She wanted to cry. She wanted to run until her lungs exploded and her heart burst from her chest, anything to soothe her mixed emotions.

"Eliza," Phillip's hand rested on her shoulder before she was even aware he'd followed her out into the night. "Are you okay?"

She nodded, sniffing as she reached up with a thumb to brush the tears off her cheek. "Mmhmm." Snow caught in her eyelashes as the wind tugged on the wisps of hair that had come loose from her plait.

He waited for a moment. She didn't respond to his touch. He moved around her, lifting her chin with his knuckle. Instead of fighting or fleeing, she walked into him, burying her face into his chest. His arms went around her out of reflex and he held her for a long moment. Heaving sobs made her body shake and he found himself rubbing her back, and leaning into her hair, speaking soft words of comfort. "It's okay. Esme's okay."

"I feel so bad," she sniffed.

"Why?"

"Alban ... he gave his life ... for me ..."

The words struck him hard. What was he supposed to say to that? He stood back from her, bracing her arms with his hand, reaching up for the fresh tear that ran down her face onto her jaw. "But ..." he struggled for words. "Oh, honey ... he was already gone ..."

Fresh tears erupted and she threatened to buckle. Eliza's breath caught in her lungs as Phillip leaned in and captured her lips with his. For a moment, she froze, eyes open, stunned at his audacity. But his lips were warm and soft and his touch so tender, and she realized she didn't mind. She'd been kissed before, but not like this. His hand snaked behind her head, fingers twisting in her hair. The other hand went to her waist, pulling her into him.

Eliza surrendered to the catharsis she found in the moment, and realized she was kissing him back. Then her logical brain kicked back into gear and she fought against what was happening between them.

She withdrew abruptly, gasping as she took a step away, their eyes locked. "Was ... was that okay?" Phillip gasped, looking horrified. His pupils were dilated and his already dark eyes were as black as pitch. "I don't know what came over me ..."

"It was more than okay," Eliza caught her breath, though her racing pulse betrayed her. "But don't ever call me *honey* again."

The Watcher appeared in the mirror behind the massive meeting table. He came with news. "The Order Operatives have been successful in their bid to obtain the Artifact of Arkanos," he announced to those assembled in the chambers of the Council of Seven.

The Father of Knowledge turned to his colleagues. "Another point for the Aegis Order," he scowled, slamming his fist onto the table. The echo reverberated through the chamber. "Where were *my* operatives? How has this been allowed to happen?"

The Father of Magic rose from his seat at the opposite end of the table. "I have chosen my champions well. And you are just a sore loser, *old friend*."

Randall sat at the work table in his office at the Archives beneath the British Museum, the *Chronicles of Arkanos* open in front of him on a stand so he could sit back and sip a cup of tea as he read. Tiberius lay on the table beside the book, napping and purring ever so softly.

Randall's eyes lifted as he scanned the room, looking for Faraday. The cat had a way of slipping off so silently Randall didn't hear him go. He could return just as silently, usually right under Randall's feet. He'd nearly tripped over the Wrens' cat on more than one occasion this week.

"Faraday," he called. "Here kitty, kitty."

There was no answer. Even Tiberius wouldn't respond to such a summons. Perhaps they thought themselves too dignified to be called like common house cats. These two felines were indeed superior to any other cat Randall had ever known. They did as they pleased and seemed content to allow Randall his own providence.

Just as he returned his attention to his book, a fracas erupted on the bookcase behind him. He turned in time to see Faraday leap from the nook where he'd hidden, his hair on end and his tail frizzed up to twice its size. Randall rose to see what was the matter, and took a step back when he realized what had appeared on the shelf beside the cat, who must have been sleeping.

Ever the skilled Archivist, he had a pair of cotton gloves in his pocket, which he donned quickly before he picked up the ancient page. The Artifact of Arkanos was sketched on the tattered parchment in dark reddish-black ink that almost seemed to glow in the fluorescent lights of the secret rooms hidden deep within the British Museum.

Randall staggered back to his chair, stunned to find this ancient document suddenly in his office. Could this possibly be from The Manifest? He lay it on the table to study it, taking out his magnifying glass to examine the ancient ink. Had Esme and Eliza been successful? Had they found the relic they were after? Had they claimed the Artifact of Arkanos for the Order? From everything he read, the ink matched. The parchment matched! *Yes!* This had to be a page from Sir Christopher Wren's Manifest! How it had gotten here, he didn't know. At this point, he didn't care! They'd done it!

Their first official field assignment was done. His work, however, was just beginning. "Faraday, old chap, you'll be happy to know your Mistress and her sister will be home before you know it. Why don't you lads wait here for her? I need to see the Grand Aegis."

EXCERPT: THE CRIMSON COMPASS

BOOK 3 OF THE MANIFEST DESTINY SERIES

Somewhere in the Aegean Sea

~360 B.C.E.

The sailor raised his weary eyes to the horizon, the sea as black as ink, and the sky just as dark. Only the dappling of stars separated the two. Still, the stars shimmered in the lifting tides, blurring the sea from the sky. Timaeus knew the sky as well as he knew the sea. Both were physical. Both were eternal.

The sailor had plenty of time to contemplate *Anima mundi*, the *soul of the world*. It was the intricate connection between all living beings. Living creatures were endowed with a soul and a reason, a mixture of sameness and difference that formed a unified, harmonious entity that permeated the Cosmos. The soul animated the universe, ensuring its rational structure and function according to *The Divine Plan*. It fed the motions of the seven planets reflecting the deep connection between mathematics and reality.

The Dēmiurgós, the *Creator* ... the One, the Many ... in their infinite wisdom, fashioned and maintained the Universe and its constant rhythm—the heartbeat of everything that lived and breathed, the balance between day and night, good and evil, heaven and hell... life and death. Same and different. *Becoming* and *Being*.

This fundamental concept challenged reality versus ideals, and tested the teachings of even the great Socrates himself. Plato, his pupil understood the plurality of gods, though Timaeus was still *becoming*.

He knew the *Dēmiurgós* fashioned and shaped the material world and was as benevolent as any of the gods might be, but he was not sure if assigning good or evil to the *Dēmiurgós* aligned with the thinking of his teacher. Before, there was only chaos, or *chōra*, until *Dēmiurgós* shaped it and constructed the universe as a single, living creature endowed with a *World Soul*, unifying all parts through proportional harmony.

The Divine Plan was not merely an account of the physical creation, but a moral and metaphysical framework that invited human beings to mirror the order of the cosmos within their own souls. Sadly, there were those who refused.

That was why the gods called the Council. They were summoned to discuss a fitting punishment for the arrogance and hubris of those who dwelled with the gods of Atlantis. Once, the favored of Poseidon, who founded it and infused it with divine order and law, the god of the sea had been forgotten and the virtue of his people eroded and fell to ambition and greed. And so, Poseidon withdrew his divine influence and left them to their own moral corruption.

Within hours, perhaps minutes, the people would face their judgement at the hand of Zeus, the most high. Poseidon himself had come to Timaeus in a dream and cautioned the teacher and philosopher of the most likely outcome. It had been the sea god himself who gave him the parcel he now kept tucked within his cloak, safe against his heart.

Poseidon had given him calm seas and gentle winds as he spirited away the most sacred treasures of Atlantis. When the earth gave way beneath the island, and the sea took back what it had made, the people would be lost, but their most significant relics would not be lost.

By the stars, he could tell the lands of Kemet would not be far. There, he would find a people already in communion with the Divine Order of the Universe. His hand went to the pouch containing two objects. Poseidon had warned Timaeus not to consider using either, but he could feel a humming and a heartbeat within, and the sea god's voice had not told him he couldn't look.

Curiosity cursed Pandora, but surely this was not the same. Cautiously, he reached into the layers of his cloak and took out the leather pouch. The cords holding it shut had swollen in the damp air and it was a struggle for his arthritic fingers to pry them open, but when he did, a small object within fell into his hand.

A crystal, as dark as obsidian, swirled with a thrumming tempo that resonated through his bones and into his core. *Lub-dub. Lub-dub.*

The entire galaxy appeared within, swirling like a whirlpool of glistening beauty, as if it had fallen from the very heavens itself. He had to force his eye away.

From the leather sack, he produced an Olivewood box, hand-carved and beautifully made. He studied the carvings, recognizing the double spiral that symbolized the journey inward. One circle for life. One for death. Then there was the star Sirius, the phases of the moon, and the flower of life, a stylized dodecagon.

The *All-Seeing Eye* appeared on the top edge as he studied it. At the latch, there was a carving of a feather crossing a heart. *Beautiful!*

On the back of the box, carefully carved in Greek were the words:

Twelve are the trials and twelve are the truths.

The heart must bear the weight.

The path must hold the light.

By the seas we walk the stars,

By the Compass, find our fate.

Timaeus's hunger to know more got the better of him. His master taught him to seek the answers in all things, and curiosity was the path to knowledge. He fumbled to find the latch, and a large circular piece of metal fell into his open palm. The disc appeared to be forged of *oreikhalkos*—a metal so precious it was considered second only to gold in value. It came only from the mines of Atlantis itself. It reminded him of copper and gold, and it caught the starlight and flashed with the red light of the cosmos. He put the crystal back in the pouch, securing it and tucking it under his arm to protect it as he studied the metallic object.

Turning it over in his wizened hands, he discovered it was a compass, but not just any compass. It was a mariner's compass, but it was a sundial as well. Beneath the outer workings, the needle spun wildly, paused then spun the other direction. He held it up, turning to find Polaris, the North Star. He held it in that direction and for a moment, the dial paused, but the spinning only resumed.

Timaeus tapped the lens, then shook it, trying to make sense of the frenzy. The humming and buzzing from inside the disc increased, and it reminded him of a panicked swarm of bees. Suddenly, he was aware of the rising and falling of the sea, as it increased. Above, clouds gathered seemingly from nowhere.

His small craft, the *Nereide*, shifted and yawed as the wind caught in his white hair and threatened to up-end the craft. He tucked the box back into the bag, tied it tightly and secured it to the single mast.

The clinker-built craft, made of cedar and cypress, waterproofed with pine resin was a sturdy craft, strong enough for solo navigation. It had ample space to store supplies for the voyage. The rounded hull was narrow, but built for speed. The keel was deep enough to navigate rivers, but provided stability in most ocean swells.

Poseidon had given it to him for the journey and it was one of the finest craft he'd ever seen. The single square sail was made of flax, dyed deep crimson, adorned with the sigil of Atlantis. Dual steering oars were secured, one on each side at the stern, and provided only a small measure of control against the sudden maelstrom.

A wave hit the craft along its starboard side and threatened to toss it into the murky depths. Were the gods angry? Was he not supposed to look? Surely there could be no harm ...

In a panic, Timaeus stood and lifted his arms to the heavens, spreading them out over the sea.

"Great Poseidon, Lord of the Deep... Father of Islands, Breaker of Ships... hear me now upon your breathless tide," he called. "I am Timaeus, son of Atlantis, lost. I am your chosen carrier of the compass that turns not to North, but to Fate! I carry the last flame of the Temple! I ask no mercy for myself, only for what I bear. If I must vanish beneath your crown of foam, at least have mercy upon all that is to be left of your once great city, Atlantis! Take me, if you must, but remember my name!"

The sea surged at him from all sides, salt and foam blinding him as he faltered, and lost his footing, stumbling across the deck as the waves dropped out from beneath the craft.

He fumbled the pouch in his panic to catch himself, the contents spilling to the deck as the ship heaved and rolled. The compass rolled to starboard, the crystal to port. "Posideon, preserve me!" he cried to the sea, and the dial of brass rolled to his feet. He clutched it into his free hand, pressing it to his chest. As the seas seemed to calm, he said, "Thank you, Sea Father. You have saved me."

But even as the words escaped his lips, a wave lifted, towering above the vessel, dropping atop the deck, sweeping the crystal into a tower of water that lifted it toward the swirling tempest. Lightning crashed around the squall as the clouds parted, opening void to the heavens. He was blinded from all but the brightest stars, but they were not the stars of a sky he knew. *I am betrayed*, the words came into his mind as the boards beneath his feet shattered and the craft began to break apart.

"*Mnēsthe tēn Atlantída*," he cried, as the waves consumed him, ship and all. His desperate plea, *Remember Atlantis*.

www.ingramcontent.com/pod-product-compliance
Lightning Source LLC
Chambersburg PA
CBHW011508170626
46812CB00009B/3023